BODYGUARD

Book 4: Ransom

Also by Chris Bradford

The Bodyguard series

Book 1: Recruit

Book 2: Hostage

Book 3: Hijack

Book 4: Ransom

Book 4: Ransom

Chris Bradford

Philomel Books

PHILOMEL BOOKS
an imprint of Penguin Random House LLC
375 Hudson Street
New York, NY 10014

First American edition published by Philomel Books in 2017. Adapted from *Ransom*, originally published in the United Kingdom by Puffin Books in 2014.

Library of Congress Cataloging-in-Publication Data is available upon request.
Printed in the United States of America.
ISBN 9781524737030
10 9 8 7 6 5 4 3 2 1

American edition edited by Brian Geffen.
American edition design by Jennifer Chung.
Text set in 11-point Palatino Nova.

To Laura, Maurizio and Andrea,

my guardians in Italy!

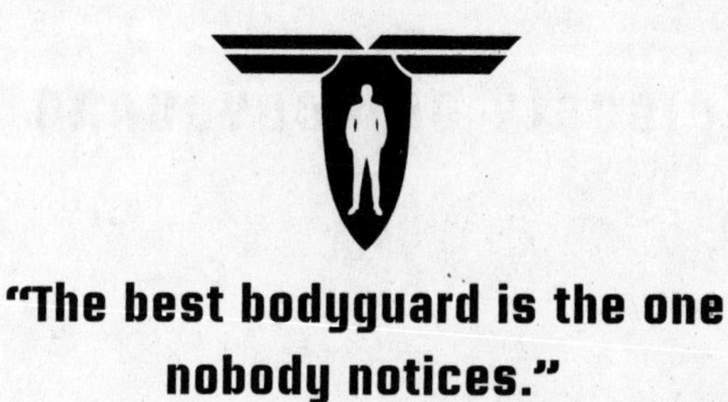

"The best bodyguard is the one nobody notices."

With the rise of teen stars, the intense media focus on celebrity families and a new wave of millionaires and billionaires, adults are no longer the only target for hostage-taking, blackmail and assassination—kids are too.

That's why they need specialized protection . . .

GUARDIAN

Guardian is a secret close-protection organization that differs from all other security outfits by training and supplying only young bodyguards.

Known as guardians, these highly skilled kids are more effective than the typical adult bodyguard, who can easily draw unwanted attention. Operating invisibly as a child's constant companion, a guardian provides the greatest possible protection for any high-profile or vulnerable young target.

In a life-threatening situation, a **guardian** is the final ring of defense.

PREVIOUSLY ON BODYGUARD . . .

Guardian recruit Connor Reeves continues to be tested to his limit . . .

Connor tapped his mic. "Alpha One to Control. Request emergency EVAC."

His earpiece burst into life and he heard Charley, Alpha team's operations leader, respond, *"Alpha One, this is Control. Backup on its way. Three minutes out."*

Three minutes? thought Connor. They'd be dead meat in that time.

Meanwhile Emily Sterling, daughter of Australian media mogul Maddox Sterling, is kidnapped and threatened . . .

"Get it over with," she muttered, willing her executioner to pull the trigger and end her suffering.

Silence.

No click. No bang. Not even a reply. Only the buzz of flies circling in the stifling heat.

What's taking him so long? Is this another one of his mind games?

But against all odds, Emily survives, and after her release, her father decides to hire Guardian to protect her and her twin sister, Chloe, on their next vacation in the Indian Ocean . . .

"Wow!" exclaimed Amir, his coffee-brown eyes widening in amazement. "That's some boat."

"That's no boat; it's a floating palace," Marc corrected as he squinted at the yacht's top deck. "It's even got a *hot tub*."

Jason shot Connor an envious glance. "You've landed a cushy assignment," he said. "Must be your reward for saving the president's daughter."

"You think so?" replied Connor, recalling the difficulties he'd faced protecting just one Principal. "I figure twins mean twice the trouble."

And Connor's initial instincts are proved right. Somali pirates are planning to hijack the yacht . . .

"What about defenses?"

Mr. Wi-Fi laughed. "It's a *pleasure* boat, Spearhead. No razor wire or water cannon. You won't be impressing us with your war stories this time."

"Where's the challenge, then?" he said with a sly grin, his teeth appearing like a crescent moon in the twilight.

Mr. Wi-Fi peered over his glasses and replied, "There isn't any. Compared with a cargo ship, the *Orchid*'s a sitting duck."

With Connor and the Sterlings unaware they're being targeted, the pirates soon locate the yacht and close in . . .

"We need to hunt like sharks," explained Spearhead. "Attack when least expected, when the prey is least ready to fight back."

His keen eyes spotted the pinpoint flash of light on the horizon. There were three more bursts in quick succession.

"That's our signal," he announced, and raised his assault rifle in the air to alert the rest of the gang.

But Connor spots the pirates' approach and rushes to warn the crew . . .

Brad ran back outside onto the upper deck, Connor close on his heels. The sun was now fully up, a burning ball of red in the dawn sky. They scanned the ocean to the *Orchid*'s stern. Half a mile directly south, five skiffs loaded with men surged across the waves.

Brad sprinted back to the captain. "Five skiffs. Pirates, by the looks of it."

"How long to contact?" asked Captain Locke.

"Less than five minutes," replied the second officer.

—

And the pirates mean to take their prize, dead or alive . . .

"They have an RPG!"

The skiff had pulled level with the bridge and the pirate was taking aim.

"I see it," replied the captain. *"Oh my—"*

His transmission cut off as the pirate launched the rocket. It scorched through the air, blazing a trail across the open water. Connor watched in wide-eyed horror as the ball of hellfire rocketed straight toward them . . .

1

The raging ball of fire, smoke and shrapnel flashed like a comet in the dawn sky. The explosion like an earsplitting clap of thunder.

For a brief moment, Connor thought the captain and everyone on the bridge had perished. Then Captain Locke's voice burst onto the radio.

"The pirates missed!" His relief was evident.

"They meant to," replied Brad, the ship's security officer. "But they won't next time."

There was a pause as the captain weighed the threat of a second RPG against the risks of ramming the skiff.

"Prepare for collision course."

Connor and Brad braced themselves. The *Orchid* sheered off to starboard just as one of the five pirate skiffs was closing in. The boat's pilot, totally unprepared for such an aggressive maneuver, tried to veer away. But it was too late. The two vessels collided at high speed. The skiff's bow crunched against the yacht's side, shattering on impact. There was a horrible screeching as the skiff scored a line down the *Orchid*'s hull. Then, like flotsam in a storm, the skiff was flipped over by the churn from the *Orchid*'s propellers, and the pirates and their weaponry were dumped into the sea.

"That'll make 'em think twice," said Brad as they watched the capsized skiff recede into the distance.

But, like stirring up a hornets' nest, the ramming only seemed to enrage the pirates more. Powering past their stranded companions who clung to the wreckage, the four surviving skiffs swarmed toward the *Orchid*.

"Why don't they give up?" asked the deckhand Jordan.

Brad gripped the rail. "They must be desperate. Nothing to lose."

The radio on his hip crackled into life.

"We have a problem," the captain announced. *"Our speed has dropped. One of the screws must have been damaged in the ramming."*

Brad turned to the crew. "Everyone. Prepare to repel boarders." He handed the empty flare gun to Connor. "Hold the fort. I'll be back in a minute."

Before Connor could question him, Brad disappeared inside the salon.

Connor peered over the gunwale. The skiffs were closing in on all sides as the *Orchid* lost headway. A ferocious burst of gunfire assaulted the upper deck. A window imploded, and he heard a scream from one of the two stewardesses stationed in the sky lounge as lookouts. Praying neither had been hurt, Connor reloaded the flare gun, at the same time wondering what the point was. A flare was a feeble match for an AK-47.

But it was all he had.

As soon as the gunfire ceased, he knelt up by the rail and took aim at the nearest skiff. The lurching of the deck made it virtually impossible to fix his target. A tall, jug-eared pirate trained his AK-47 on him. But Connor squeezed his trigger first. The flare *whoosh*ed from the barrel. A bright red ball of flame shot across the waves . . . and fell short.

Connor briefly saw the flare extinguish itself in the waves, before he dove to the deck as a hail of bullets peppered the stern gunwale.

So much for my attempt at fending off the pirates.

Brad reappeared by his side, now in possession of a stainless-steel 12-gauge pump-action shotgun. "Time to fight fire with fire!"

Connor stared in disbelief at the fearsome weapon. "I thought you said guns were illegal."

Brad checked the chamber, then clicked off the safety catch. "Only in port," he replied with a grim smile, and he took aim over the gunwale.

The blast of the shotgun was deafening. Connor held his hands over his ears as Brad fired again and again. Then he dropped back down beside him.

"Did you hit anyone?" asked Connor as another strafing of bullets cut into the *Orchid*.

Brad shook his head. "I'm trying to knock out their engines," he explained, rapidly reloading.

On the port side, Jordan and another deckhand, Kieran, threw a storage net into the sea to entangle the outboards of an approaching skiff. But as they were launching the net, a clatter of gunfire punctured the air. Jordan was thrown backward. Blood splattered across the salon's glass doors.

Connor rushed to his aid. Jordan slumped to the deck, groaning, blood pouring from the bullet wound in his shoulder. Kieran ripped off his T-shirt and handed it to Connor.

"Apply pressure. I'll get the first-aid kit."

As Kieran ran inside, Connor pressed the balled-up T-shirt against the wound. Jordan cried out.

"You'll be all right," assured Connor, not knowing what else to say. "I promise you, I've had worse."

Even through the haze of pain, Jordan managed a weak smile of disbelief.

Blasts like thunder echoed off the blood-smeared glass as Brad fired his shotgun in angry retaliation. But the pirates showed no sign of retreat. Bullets ripped through the air, and the roar of their outboard motors buzzed like angry wasps.

"Did the net . . . stop . . . them?" asked Jordan through clenched teeth as Kieran reappeared with the first-aid kit.

Looking to the stern, Connor spotted the net floating away on the *Orchid*'s wake.

"No," he said, shaking his head in dismay.

Without warning, a grappling hook latched itself to the port-side rail. Connor saw the line go taut. The pirates were boarding the *Orchid*.

2

The buzzing woke Amir. He yawned and glanced at his watch: 03:30.

Why had he set his alarm for so early?

As he rubbed the sleep from his eyes, the alarm continued its incessant buzzing. He reached over to switch it off and promptly fell to the floor. Dazed, Amir looked around the darkened briefing room and at his upturned chair. Of course, he wasn't in bed. He was on night duty, supposedly monitoring Operation Gemini.

The buzzing grew more urgent, and Amir scrambled up to his desk. On the glowing computer screen a Red Alert icon was flashing. Clicking on the pulsing box, he stared at the few stark lines of text, then grabbed his phone.

"What is it, Amir?" Charley answered drowsily.

"Distress call from the *Orchid.*"

There was a moment's silence as the words sank in. Then she replied, "I'll be right down," her voice sharp and alert.

A short while later, Charley wheeled herself through the door, wearing a T-shirt and sweatpants.

"What information do we have?"

Amir nodded to his computer screen. "The *Orchid* sent out a DSC distress signal at 0625 hours, Seychelles local time. It gave her position as two hundred and forty nautical miles east-northeast of Mahé."

"Do we know the actual problem?"

Amir swallowed anxiously. "Pirates."

Charley looked at him. "Seems like you've lost your bet with Ling," she said, her tone bereft of humor. "Any communication from Connor?"

Amir shook his head. "The distress signal was picked up by the Seychelles Maritime Rescue Coordination Center. Since the *Orchid*'s out of range for VHF radio and cell phones, a satellite call is the only possible option. But there's no mention of it in this report."

Charley picked up the phone. "I'll contact the Seychelles coast guard for an update. In the meantime, wake Colonel Black, then see if you can get through to Connor via your SOS app."

3

Connor shouted a warning to Brad, but the repeated blasts of the shotgun had temporarily deafened him. Leaving Kieran to tend to Jordan, Connor ran to the rail. Inside his polo-shirt pocket his phone buzzed with a message. He ignored it. A pirate was attempting to scale the knotted rope, the bucking skiff making his progress slow but certain.

Connor pulled the flare gun from his hip pocket. He took aim, then realized it was unloaded. He fumbled for another flare from the clip, but in his hurry he dropped them, and they scattered across the deck. He frantically retrieved one. Snapping open the breach, he pushed the flare home, then clicked it shut. Just as he went to take aim again, the chef rushed onto the deck, wielding a flaming bottle of spirits.

"My own special pirate cocktail!" he shouted as he launched it at the skiff below.

The bottle shattered across the bow, spreading a sea of flame along the wooden skiff. The pirates screamed and scrambled away from the blaze. In his panic the pilot veered sharply, jerking on the grappling rope and catapulting his comrade into the ocean.

Then a wave broke over the skiff, dousing the fire. The pirates, quickly recovering from the shock attack, made another approach. They powered toward the *Orchid,* leaving their fellow pirate to drown.

But the chef had plenty more bottles where that one had come from and reappeared moments later with two more Molotov cocktails.

On the starboard side, Brad fired his shotgun again. This time he hit his mark. The outboard engines of the targeted skiff sputtered and choked, smoke spewing from their exhausts. But the pilot had also been caught in the hail of buckshot. He slumped over the tiller of his outboard and sent the boat swerving off course.

"Two down!" said Brad grimly as he sheltered behind the gunwale.

Despite their losses, the pirates refused to give up. Two of the skiffs now made simultaneous attacks on the *Orchid*'s bow. The crew up front called for help, and Brad and Chef rushed to their aid. But, with everyone committed to the port and starboard attacks, no one noticed the stern assault by the third skiff.

Only Connor heard the clang of a grappling hook on the rail. He spun around to see a colossal pirate, an assault rifle strapped across his back, standing on the skiff's bow like a figurehead. The ease with which he rode the turbulent waves was unnerving. Beckoning to his pilot to move closer to the *Orchid*'s stern, the pirate was preparing to make his leap.

Connor had only one shot. He couldn't afford to miss this time.

The flare rocketed the short distance and struck home. Just as he had planned, it landed beside the fuel canister for the outboard. The pilot shouted in terror and jumped over the side as a spark ignited the diesel. Showered in flaming fuel, the other pirates leaped for their lives. The skiff then exploded in a massive fireball, a plume of black smoke rising into the air like a mushroom cloud. Connor shielded his eyes from the blast. And when he looked again, the skiff was sinking rapidly beneath the waves.

But the pirate who'd leaped from the bow still clung on to the rope. Like some monster of the deep, he hauled himself up through the rushing water toward the *Orchid*'s stern. Connor couldn't believe the man's strength, or his crazed determination.

The hook was pulled tight against the rail, and Connor had no hope of wrenching it free. He raced through the salon to the galley. There, he grabbed a fire extinguisher and snatched a carving knife from the chef's block. By the time he'd sprinted back, the pirate had reached the stern and was clambering up the tender garage's huge bay door.

Pulling the safety pin from the extinguisher, Connor let loose a jet of white foam, turning the bay door slick and oily. The pirate scrambled to gain purchase with his feet and thumped hard into the fiberglass hull. Foam glistened off his rippling torso, and rivulets of water ran down his smooth bullet-shaped head.

Yet still he held on.

Discarding the empty extinguisher, Connor took up the knife. The pirate snarled like a wild beast when he saw Connor furiously sawing at his rope. With grim determination, the pirate climbed hand over hand. The rope started to fray, but Connor knew he'd never cut through in time. The pirate was already halfway up. Then the *Orchid* struck the swell hard, and the pirate lost his grip and slipped down to the waterline. Only his Herculean strength prevented him from losing all hold on the rope.

The pirate heaved himself back up as Connor continued to slice frantically at the fraying fibers. The pirate's fingers reached for the deck. The rope finally parted . . . and Connor watched the man tumble back into the foaming sea.

4

"This is definitely a new breed of pirates," said Brad as the *Orchid*'s crew recovered in the salon.

After their joint attack had failed, the remaining pirates had finally given up their pursuit and the *Orchid* had escaped, bullet-ridden but unbreached. Jordan had been moved to a guest bedroom, his wound dressed and painkillers administered. Kathy, the second stewardess, was being treated for minor cuts from the shattered window.

"I've never known so many skiffs to hunt together as a pack, or seen such firepower," Brad continued as he paced the room, still holding his shotgun. "Their outboards were brand-new too, top of the line."

"But how did they even find us?" asked Connor, standing near Emily and Chloe, who huddled together on one of the sofas. "It's not as if we're in the transit corridor or cruising the Somalian coast."

"That's a good point," agreed Captain Locke, looking to

Brad for an answer. "We're almost as far from the mainland as we can be."

Brad shrugged. "Who knows? It might just be bad luck that we crossed paths with the pirates. This distance from Somalia, they have to be operating from a mother ship. *Unless* . . . they're on a one-way mission, which could explain their reckless determination to attack us."

"So are we safe now?" asked Amanda, who sat in a leather chair, her foot tapping nervously on the carpet. At some point, Mr. Sterling's ever glamorous fiancée had managed to apply makeup, although her eyes were still glassy with shock.

Brad studied the shotgun in his hand, then glanced toward the open ocean at their stern. "It's highly unlikely the pirates will make another attempt. But I'll feel more comfortable when we're in safe harbor."

"And how long will that be?"

"Another forty-eight hours," announced the captain.

"What about Jordan?" asked Sophie. "Kieran may be trained to give first aid, but he's no doctor."

"It looks worse than it is, Soph," replied Brad. "I've checked the wound. The bullet passed straight through. But you're right; he does need medical attention."

"Our plan is to cas-evac Jordan as soon as we're within helicopter range," explained the captain. "We've retracted our distress signal, but requested medical help to be at the—"

"Sorry for interrupting, Captain," said Chief Officer Fielding, rushing in from the bridge, "but we've picked up a Mayday call."

"From the pirates, I hope," the chef said, laughing. He was busy behind the bar preparing more explosive bottles in case the pirates returned.

"No, a Dutch yacht," replied the chief officer, his expression short of humor beneath his beard. "Engine failure caused by a fire. Four people on board. They're requesting urgent assistance."

"How far are they from our current position?" asked the captain.

"They're nine nautical miles southeast."

"Surely you can't be thinking of going to their rescue," said Kieran. "We have enough problems of our own."

Captain Locke gave him a stern look. "I'm well aware of that. But we're legally obliged to help."

"Can't another vessel respond?" asked Amanda.

The chief officer shook his head. "There doesn't appear to be anyone else in the vicinity."

"Then set a course for the stranded yacht," the captain ordered.

"But the pirates!" exclaimed Scott.

"Exactly. And if they've picked up the distress call too, they'll be like vultures on carrion. So keep a sharp lookout."

5

Connor scanned the horizon, the binoculars pulling the waves farthest away into detail. Small white crests like feathers rippled on the ocean's surface, but there were no pirates in sight. The empty sea was almost as disconcerting as it was reassuring.

"Do you want your breakfast now?" asked Emily, her face slightly pale from the aftershock of the attack.

Connor's stomach growled. "That would be great. Fending off pirates is hard work!"

Emily smiled weakly, then disappeared inside. Connor leaned against the rail and felt his bulked-up phone in the top pocket of his shirt. Only now did he remember he'd received a text message during the hijack attempt. He was surprised his phone had a signal so far out at sea. Then he saw the text had been delivered via Amir's SOS app, which allowed short bursts of satellite communication. He replied with a simple message:

All clear. But responding to another yacht's mayday.

A moment after he sent the text, a muffled shriek rose from within the yacht. Connor moved like lightning. The cry had come from the direction of the galley. He bounded down the stairs and found Emily standing outside in the corridor. Trembling but, to his relief, apparently unharmed.

"There's someone in there," she whispered, nodding to the galley.

"One of the crew?" asked Connor.

Emily shook her head. "I don't think so. It happened so quickly—a flash out of the corner of my eye as I opened the door—but I definitely saw someone."

"Stay here," he said. Twisting the handle, Connor pushed open the door with his shoulder, keeping his hands free in case he needed to defend himself. *Could a pirate have hidden away during the attack?*

The galley's sleek white kitchen shone in the bright glare of the overhead lights. The gleaming marble worktop was clear, save for the chef's block of knives stowed in one corner, a stainless-steel toaster, an espresso machine and a large bowl of fruit.

Conner poked his head farther around the door, but there was no one there.

"Perhaps you imagined it?" he said, stepping inside and giving the room a once-over.

Emily followed a hesitant step behind him. "I'm sure I saw something move. Do you think it might have been a . . . rat?"

Connor laughed. "On *this* yacht? It must have high-class tastes."

"Then why's your breakfast missing?" asked Emily.

Connor glanced over at the tray on the serving counter. His orange juice had been drunk, and crumbs were all that remained of his buttered toast.

"Perhaps it was Scott or one of the other crew," suggested Connor, although he wasn't convinced himself.

"Or my sister," said Emily, her tone hopeful. "I know she's a secret snacker. She always denies it—"

Connor held up his hand, silencing her. On the floor outside the door to the walk-in freezer lay a trail of crumbs. Whoever had been helping themselves to his breakfast had been in a hurry.

His sixth sense started twitching.

Sliding a chef's knife out from its block, Connor silently approached the walk-in freezer. Emily stood motionless, not even daring to breathe. Grasping the handle, Connor raised the knife and steeled himself to open the door.

6

"Don't hurt me!" cried a pitiful voice as Connor flung open the freezer door.

Shivering in the chill air crouched a skinny boy, his teeth chattering, his eyes wide with fear.

Connor noticed he was concealing something in his fist. "Hands where I can see them," he ordered, pointing the knife at him.

The boy raised two stick-thin arms. He held a piece of toast in one hand and an apple in the other.

At least they aren't lethal weapons, thought Connor. He eyed the boy, who wore a pair of tattered shorts and a UNICEF T-shirt, his bare feet curled up on the cold freezer floor.

"Who are you?" Connor demanded.

"Cali," said the boy in almost a whisper.

"Pirate?"

Cali shook his head firmly. "No, no! Not pirate!"

"Then how did you get on board?"

"I from Somalia." Cali offered a broad smile, his uneven teeth appearing pearl white against his midnight skin.

Connor narrowed his eyes and took a step closer with the knife. "I asked you a question. Now answer me."

The smile vanished, and the boy cowered away from him.

"Take it easy, Connor," said Emily, breaking from her paralysis and hurrying over. "Can't you see he's terrified?"

Connor glanced at the formidable blade in his hand, then back at the trembling boy. He supposed he was quite a fearsome sight, but given the circumstances, he had to make a show of force. He patted the boy down—he wasn't concealing any weapons and didn't appear to be an immediate physical threat, so Connor lowered the knife.

"Hi, I'm Emily." Easing past Connor, she bent down and offered her hand to the boy. "Don't be scared. I'm your friend."

Cali hesitantly took it and stood up. His legs were scrawny, the bones more prominent than muscle, and his face hollow cheeked. But he wore a ready smile.

"Thank you, Emily," said the boy, still keeping a wary distance from Connor as she led him over to the serving bar.

"Are you hungry?" she asked.

Cali nodded. Emily went over and opened the stainless-steel fridge. The chef had left a tantalizing array of midnight snacks—sandwiches, fresh pineapple, cheeses and luxury chocolates, along with a jug of fresh orange juice. Emily took them out and placed them on the serving bar, then fetched a couple of plates and glasses from an overhead cabinet. Cali's eyes were already devouring the food laid out before him. Emily passed him a fresh tuna sandwich and he bit into it ravenously, chewing fast and swallowing quickly as if worried the food would be snatched away at any second.

Connor wasn't willing to accept him so readily. He kept the chef's knife to hand and stayed close to Emily, his eye ever watchful for any threatening move from their stowaway. Connor judged Cali to be only a little younger than himself. His hair was a tight knit of black curls. And across Cali's raw-boned arms, Connor noticed a patchwork of thin pale scars like scratches, only deeper. Yet despite the boy's feeble appearance, Connor had to assume for now that the stowaway was capable of anything.

As Cali ate, Connor persisted with his questioning. "How did you get on this yacht?"

"The gangway. It down in Mahé," Cali replied through a mouthful of sandwich.

"Yesterday?" Connor knew Brad had kept a careful watch throughout their unscheduled stopover.

Cali shook his head. "No, before."

Connor frowned. "You mean, you've been on this yacht for over a week?" He found that hard to believe.

Cali bit into his apple with a loud crunch and nodded enthusiastically. "I go to South Africa."

"South Africa?" Emily laughed. "But we're on our way to the Maldives."

Cali furrowed his brow and studied the apple intensely before looking up. "Maldives near South Africa?"

"No, a long way off," she replied as she poured Connor a glass of orange juice and passed him a sandwich too. Cali chewed his lower lip in disappointment. "What made you think we were going to South Africa?" asked Emily.

"I saw South African flag on man cleaning deck," he replied.

"Oh, you mean Jordan," she said, a shadow passing across her face as she mentioned the injured deckhand's name. "Yes, he's from Cape Town. And he's always wearing that T-shirt. Very proud of his country."

As Emily continued chatting with Cali, Connor fell deep into thought, barely tasting the sandwich he was eating. How come none of the crew had seen this boy? He and Brad had done a full security sweep before departing. There was no way they could have missed him.

There was only one reasonable explanation: the boy had to be lying.

"Where have you been hiding?" Connor interrupted.

Cali pointed beneath their feet. "Underneath small boat."

"*Underneath?* But we've used the tender every day."

"No, under deck."

Connor tried to picture the tender garage. He vaguely recalled Brad pointing out a small hatch near the locker area that led to the bilge, a sealed compartment in the lower hull where water, oil and other noxious liquids collected. Not exactly a pleasant place to hide.

"How come you speak English?" asked Emily cheerily.

Pride lit up Cali's eyes. "My father. He a teacher."

"So why are you trying to get to South Africa?" said Connor.

"No future in Somalia. No family."

"But what about your father?"

The smile dropped from Cali's face. "He dead."

Emily put a hand to her mouth. "Oh, that's terrible! You have no one?"

Cali's gaze fell to the floor and he shook his head sadly.

Knowing the heart-rending pain losing a father caused, Connor felt his resistance to the boy momentarily weaken. "What happened?"

"Pirates attack his fishing boat—"

"But you said he was a teacher."

Cali put aside the apple, seeming to have lost his appetite. "He was. But there no school. Too much war. So he become fisherman, like my grandfather."

"Why would the pirates attack a *fisherman*?" asked Connor.

"For his boat. They slit his throat. Then force me to join them. They whip me." Cali held up his scarred arms. "But Seychelles coast guard catch us. I escape. Now I try get to South Africa for better life."

Emily looked over at Connor, her eyes glassy with tears.

Connor could see that her own traumatic experiences made her empathize with Cali. "We have to help him somehow."

Connor studied the Somali boy sitting beside them. He too sympathized with the boy's plight—if it were true. His life sounded horrific, and in any other circumstance he would try to help. But Connor's first duty was to protect Emily and Chloe. And this boy was still an unknown quantity.

A potential threat.

"He's a security risk. A possible pirate. I have to tell the captain."

"Must you?" implored Emily.

"Yes, he bloody well must," said Brad, storming into the galley and seizing the boy.

7

"If he has been on board for a week, that at least explains how the pirates found us," said Brad. "The boy must have been sending them our coordinates."

Head bowed and shoulders slumped, Cali stood surrounded by the captain, Brad, Scott and Connor in the center of the salon.

"But how?" asked Emily, who perched on the sofa next to her sister and Amanda. "Cali couldn't exactly walk onto the bridge and use your radio."

"She's got a point," said Chloe.

"A portable GPS comms unit, most likely," explained Brad. "We'll need to search his supposed hiding place. Although I find it hard to believe he hid in the bilge."

Scott seized the boy by the scruff of his neck. "We should throw this piece of scum overboard."

Cali stared back in wide-eyed alarm. "I know nothing. I not pirate!" he protested.

"Of course you are," said Scott, shaking Cali like a bag of bones. "And it's all your fault my friend's been shot!"

"Stop!" cried Emily, jumping up from her seat. "You can't blame Cali for that."

Scott turned on her. "Oh yes, I can. Don't you think it's a little coincidental that this Somali boy appeared at the same time as the pirates?"

"He's trying to *escape* the pirates," explained Emily. "His father was killed by them."

Scott rolled his eyes to the ceiling. "And you *believe* his sob story? He's lying to save his skin. If he didn't signal the pirates, then he climbed on board during the attack. He's guilty either way."

"No! No! Not true!" cried Cali, struggling in Scott's grip. "I do nothing."

Captain Locke put a hand on Scott's shoulder. "Let the boy go, Scott. He didn't shoot Jordan. Another pirate did."

"He's *not* a pirate," insisted Emily as Scott reluctantly released Cali and backed away, fuming.

"Whether he's a pirate or not, the consequences of having a stowaway are grave," said Captain Locke, eyeing Cali with distrust.

"Can't we just drop him off in the Maldives?" suggested Amanda, still reclined on the sofa, an ice-cold drink in her hand.

"No. As soon as this boy boarded the *Orchid*, he became

our legal responsibility. We'll have to arrange for him to be deported to his country. And the cost in terms of time, money and legal fees is significant. Mr. Sterling will *not* be pleased."

"I don't want go back to Somalia," said Cali, crossing his arms defiantly.

"You keep quiet," said the captain, jabbing a finger at him. "You've caused enough trouble as it is." He turned to Brad. "We'll hand him over to the authorities as soon as we dock, but in the meantime, confine him to a cabin for the rest of the voyage."

Nodding, Brad took Cali by the arm.

"He should be arrested," said Scott bitterly. "Put in jail where he belongs."

Captain Locke fixed Scott with a stare. "We can't jump to any conclusions without proof."

"What proof do you need? He just appeared out of thin air, right after we were attacked. What else is he but a pirate?"

"The authorities will deal with him appropriately. Now get back to your duties."

"Please! Can't Cali just stay on the yacht?" said Emily, appealing to the captain. "I'll ask my father to send the *Orchid* to South Africa after the vacation."

The captain shook his head. "That's not how it works, Emily. If port officials discover him on board, *we*—as in myself and the rest of the crew—could face legal actions for allowing it. Furthermore, as Connor pointed out, he's a security risk."

"But he's got no family," Emily pressed. "There's no future for him in Somalia."

The captain held up his hand. "I'm sorry, Emily, that's just the way it is."

As Brad led Cali away, Connor noticed a small bulge in the back of the boy's shorts. Somehow Connor had missed the spot while patting down the boy.

"Wait!" cried Connor. He stepped over to Cali and pulled out a small flashlight from the boy's back pocket. For a while, he'd felt sorry for the boy, and he'd even started to believe he was an innocent stowaway. But this changed everything. "He's one of them—a pirate!"

"Me?" said Cali, his mouth falling open in shock. "N-no, not I."

"If we need proof, this is it," declared Connor, glaring at the boy. "I saw a flashing light on deck this morning. Cali signaled the pirates with this."

"No, I use it for hiding place. Very dark," Cali pleaded. His eyes flicked nervously between his captors.

Scott looked like he might tear the boy limb from limb.

Then the chief officer strode into the salon. "Captain, the Dutch yacht is in sight."

8

Connor focused his binoculars on the Dutch yacht drifting a couple of nautical miles to their port bow. Roughly half the size of the *Orchid*, the sleek pearl-white boat was still an impressive sight. There was no one on deck, giving the unsettling impression of a ghost ship. Yet, with only four crew members, Connor realized they'd all be below, dealing with the engine fire.

The atmosphere on the *Orchid* herself was tense. While key personnel carried out essential duties on the bridge, the majority of the crew stood watch—except for Scott, who was keeping a close guard over Cali in a cabin below deck, and Kieran, who was tending to the injured Jordan. Chloe and Emily sat in the sky lounge, ostensibly playing a silent game of cards but their gaze actually toward the drifting yacht. Sophie waited on Amanda in the salon, the model flicking through a pile of glossy magazines, another ice-cold drink in her hand.

Brad appeared on the upper deck and joined Connor at the aft rail. His shotgun rested on his shoulder, the weapon now a permanent accessory. "The captain's just hailed the yacht. Any sign of the pirates?"

Connor shook his head. "Nothing." He kept his eyes fixed on the yacht. He was still annoyed with himself for letting his guard down with the pirate boy.

"They're probably still licking their wounds," said Brad, the corner of his mouth curling into a grin.

As the *Orchid* made its final approach, Connor could make out the name on the side of the hull: *Sunriser*. A man wearing a white peaked cap and jacket appeared on the yacht's main deck and waved. Brad raised his hand in acknowledgment.

The *Orchid* decreased speed and came alongside the disabled vessel.

Captain Locke stepped from the bridge and saluted the other captain. "Ahoy there! Captain Locke at your service."

The Dutch captain returned his salute. The man's face was haggard, his eyes sunken, and a few days of stubble coated his chin. Considering they'd come to his rescue, the Dutch captain didn't look very pleased to see them. He bowed his head. "I'm so sorry."

"What have you to apologize for?" said Captain Locke, his brow creasing in puzzlement. "We're only too happy to come to your assistance."

But the answer emerged from the yacht's dark interior: a mighty warrior of a man armed with an AK-47.

Connor could scarcely believe his eyes. It was the pirate who'd tumbled from the *Orchid*'s stern.

Brad instinctively brought his shotgun down to fire.

"DON'T!" shouted the pirate, pressing the barrel of his rifle to the Dutch captain's head. "I'll kill him."

Brad faltered in his attack. The Dutch captain stood motionless, what little color left in his face draining completely away as his life hung in the balance.

"Throw your weapon over the side," the pirate ordered Brad.

Connor could see Brad weighing the options. His first duty was to protect the crew and passengers of the *Orchid*. But he couldn't be held responsible for the death of an innocent man either. With great reluctance, Brad tossed his only weapon into the sea.

A roar of outboard engines suddenly cut through the air as two skiffs powered out of the yacht's shadow and surrounded the *Orchid*.

"We underestimated you," said the pirate. "I won't do so again."

He spun the AK-47 toward Brad and blasted him in the chest.

9

"That's for killing my cousin," snarled the pirate, ceasing his burst of violence.

Brad slumped to the deck, blood pouring from multiple wounds. Connor rushed to his side, but could see the damage was catastrophic.

"C-c-citadel," gasped Brad.

Connor tried to pick him up and drag him to safety.

"No . . ." Brad groaned, gripping Connor's hand with the last of his strength. "Get the girls—" His eyes rolled back in his head, and his body shuddered, then fell deathly still.

"Brad!" cried Connor, trying to revive his friend and mentor.

Another gunshot rang out, its deafening blast making Connor cower in terror. He glanced over the rail. The Dutch captain lay at the pirate's feet, his body twitching, blood pooling around his head. In the water below, a skiff docked alongside the *Orchid*, grappling hooks and ladders latched on like claws, and pirates surged up the ropes.

This is going to be a slaughter, Connor realized with horror. With their comrades killed in action, the pirates wanted more than just to hijack—they wanted revenge.

Having no time to mourn Brad, Connor ducked down and sprinted along the far side of the yacht. The rest of the *Orchid*'s crew knew the drill and were already running for their lives.

Connor burst into the sky lounge.

"What's happening?" Chloe shrieked, their cards scattered across the table. "We heard gunfire."

"Brad's been shot. Pirates."

"No . . . not again. It can't be happening!" cried Emily, collapsing to the floor at the sight of Brad's blood smeared over Connor's clothes.

"Back to the citadel. *Now!*" said Connor, pulling the distraught Emily to her feet and grabbing Chloe by the wrist. He bundled them down the stairs as fast as he could.

They met Kieran and Scott dragging Jordan out of the guest bedroom. Sophie was dashing ahead down the corridor with Amanda.

"Where's everyone going?" asked Cali, running after them.

"Safe room," cried Emily, almost tripping over her sister's heels. "Come with us."

They passed the staircase leading to the lower deck. Outside they could hear urgent shouts, the language strange and unintelligible to Connor's ears.

"Hurry!" urged the captain, who was waiting at the entrance to the galley. He shepherded Amanda and Sophie through the narrow doorway and toward the crew's quarters.

But, as Kieran and Scott tried to manhandle the injured Jordan through, a bottleneck formed and panic ensued.

"Not you, pirate boy!" said Scott, kicking Cali away.

The boy tumbled to the floor and was trampled underfoot.

Emily tried to help him up, but her efforts were cut short as a devilish face appeared at a nearby porthole.

Chloe screamed. A gunshot went off.

Like the baying of a pack of dogs, the pirates' whoops and cries could be heard closing in. Connor noticed the door leading to the outside deck start to open. Realizing they'd never all make it to the citadel in time, he shoved Emily and Chloe into the captain's arms and rushed back down the corridor.

"NO!" barked the captain.

But Connor was committed to the sacrifice. He launched himself into a flying kick just as a large head with jug ears poked inside. Connor's foot struck the back of the door, slamming it against the frame and crushing the pirate in the jamb. The pirate howled in pain and fury before retracting his bruised head from its viselike grip. Connor threw his weight against the door and turned the lock. The pirate could be heard hammering furiously on the other side.

"Come on, Connor," said the captain, holding the galley door open for him.

Connor could see Emily and Chloe were through and heading for the safety of the citadel. He was the only one left—aside from Cali, who was struggling back to his feet. As he ran for the galley, a burst of gunfire erupted behind him. Connor heard the lock shattering and the door being kicked open.

"Joogso!" shouted the pirate. *"Istaag ama waan ku tooganayaa."*

Connor had no idea what the man was saying, but he wasn't going to stop for anyone.

"STOP! He kill us!" cried Cali, holding up his hand and getting in Connor's way.

Glancing over his shoulder, Connor saw the jug-eared pirate leveling his AK-47 at him. As the pirate depressed the trigger, Connor shoved Cali aside but was too late to save himself. A bullet clipped his upper arm, spinning him around. A second bullet struck him in the chest, and he tumbled down the staircase, landing in a heap at the bottom and lying there, silent and motionless.

10

Captain Locke sealed the bulkhead door. There was a *clunk* as the heavy-duty lock engaged. The door to the citadel wouldn't be opened again for anything but rescue.

"Where's Connor?" Emily asked as the captain descended the stairs into the crew's compact living quarters that doubled as the yacht's citadel. The combined kitchen–dining room was cramped with nine crew members and three guests. Kieran and Scott were settling the groaning Jordan into one of the tiny bunk beds while the others huddled around the small dining table. An atmosphere of barely restrained hysteria hung in the air.

Captain Locke addressed the survivors, his expression solemn. "Connor didn't make it."

"What do you mean, *he didn't make it*?" said Emily, rising from the bench and clutching the table for support. "He's still out there! So's Cali. We have to open the door!"

The captain rested a hand on her shoulder. "No. I saw Connor get shot. He's dead."

Emily sank back onto the bench. "This can't be happening..."

She stared mutely at the cabin wall, tears welling in her eyes in silent grief. Overwhelmed by the sudden loss, Chloe gave a grieved cry, then fell forward and buried her head in her arms.

"What about Brad?" asked Sophie in a tiny, hesitant voice.

Captain Locke shook his head sadly. Sophie collapsed into sobs, Kathy pulling her into an embrace, letting her friend weep on her shoulder.

From the stairwell, the harsh clank of metal on metal rang out. All eyes turned fearfully toward the sound.

"Don't worry," said Captain Locke. "They can't get through."

"So what now?" asked Amanda, her lips thin, the makeup no longer hiding the strain. "We're trapped."

"We sit tight and await rescue."

"From *who* exactly? *He* said"—she pointed to the chief officer almost as if in accusation—"there aren't any other boats in the area."

"NATO's navy task force," replied the captain, trying his best to maintain his composure and authority despite the desperate situation. "Danny, send out a Mayday on the radio. See who you can contact."

The chief officer nodded and went over to the small console in the corner of the room.

"I won't lie to you," said the captain, leaning forward and resting his palms on the table. "Rescue could be anything from a day to a week away. We may have to prepare for even longer. The key thing is to remain focused and positive. Chef, I want you to make a full inventory of our food and water supplies. Geoff, check our power situation and what reserve batteries we have access to. Kathy and Sophie, I need you to organize the bunk rooms and a watch duty rota. Kieran, take stock of our first-aid supplies and attend to Jordan with—"

"Captain," interrupted Danny, his tone grave. "The radio's dead."

Captain Locke frowned. "Have you tried all the channels?"

The chief officer nodded. "I even checked the battery connection."

"Let me have a look," said Geoff, the engineer, getting up from the table to inspect. After testing a series of buttons, he opened the front panel. He glanced over his shoulder at the captain, a dark look in his eyes. "Somebody's sabotaged it."

Scott punched the wall in fury. "That little rat of a stowaway! If I ever get my hands on him again, I'll wring his scrawny neck."

"So we're . . . cut off from rescue?" uttered Amanda, clasping her hands tightly together to stop their trembling.

"Not exactly," said Chief Officer Fielding, managing a reassuring smile through his beard. "I triggered the emergency position–indicating radio beacon as I left the bridge."

11

"Shut that thing down," ordered Spearhead, pointing to the flashing light atop the EPIRB unit.

Big Mouth rushed across the bridge to the bracket-mounted beacon and searched for the button that Mr. Wi-Fi had shown him on the laptop diagram. The emergency instructions meant nothing to him, but he found the red circle and pressed it. The light went dead.

Spearhead picked up the radio from the comms unit. Mimicking the BBC World Service newscaster to whom he'd listened while learning English, he said in a gruff British accent, "All stations, all stations, all stations. This is motor yacht *Orchid*. Our position is . . ." He paused briefly, checking the GPS. "South two degrees, forty-one minutes, forty-two seconds; East sixty-two degrees, fifty-four minutes, nineteen seconds. Alongside Dutch yacht *Sunriser*. Engine fire extinguished. No further danger to crew. Cancel our EPIRB distress alert. I repeat, cancel our distress alert."

Spearhead waited for a response. He received nothing but static.

This was good news, for it meant there were no other ships in the immediate vicinity. Any Mayday calls the *Orchid* might have made by radio would have fallen on deaf ears. But he understood that the EPIRB worked differently and wasn't limited by range. Before leaving on their mission, Mr. Wi-Fi had explained that the unit transmitted a signal every fifty seconds via satellite. The yacht's identity and position would have already been received by a Maritime Rescue Coordination Center, who'd have forwarded the data to the Seychelles or Kenyan coast guard. Once a satellite picked up an EPIRB signal, the whole process could take less than a minute.

Spearhead knew he and his men were racing against the clock. The authorities would have their position to within three nautical miles and would soon launch a search-and-rescue operation. Either the distress alert had to be canceled or they needed to be long gone by the time any rescue team arrived.

He broadcast the message again. Still no response. Replacing the handset, he spotted the satellite phone farther along the console. This would guarantee cancellation—if he could find the right number. As he reached over for the receiver, Spearhead noticed Big Mouth plonking himself into the captain's chair and planting his feet on the control panel.

"Get off! I'm the captain around here," Spearhead snarled, jabbing a thumb at his chest.

Big Mouth unwillingly eased himself from the leather seat as Juggs stormed onto the bridge. "The crew are holed up in the bow."

Spearhead spun on him in irritation. "Well, break the door down."

Juggs shrugged ineffectually. "We can't. It's steel. Locked from the inside."

Spearhead scowled. This problem would cause a serious delay. Without the *Orchid*'s captain or his crew, he couldn't sail the super-yacht—not with his knuckleheaded men, anyway. Spearhead cursed himself for shooting the Dutch captain, but his bloodlust had gotten the better of him. Then he remembered the equipment he'd spotted in the loading bay of the Dutch yacht.

"There's a blowtorch aboard the other boat," he said. "Get it."

Spearhead turned to Big Mouth, who was now randomly pressing buttons on the bridge console and watching the lights flash. "Stop that! Take four men and search this yacht. Bring any hostages to me. If we can't cut through, we'll need an incentive to *make* them open the door."

12

Connor's fingers twitched as he slowly came to. The back of his head throbbed where it had struck the bottom step. His left arm felt as heavy as lead, almost like he'd been punched in one spot repeatedly. And he was struggling to breathe; his chest felt compressed, his ribs bruised. But he was alive.

His eyes flickered open. The soft glow of the overhead lights appeared harsh and glaring to him, intensifying his pounding headache. Connor glanced down at his chest. There was no blood. But there was a ragged black hole in his polo shirt where the bullet had penetrated. He had no idea how he'd survived. The high-tech fabric was intended to stop only rounds from a handgun, not a 7.62 mm high-velocity shot from an assault rifle.

As Connor sat up, wincing with pain, there was a tinkle of glass in his breast pocket. He pulled out the remains of his smartphone, the bullet still embedded in the screen. He almost laughed in disbelief. He'd been saved not only by the pocket's double layer of bulletproof fabric but by the phone absorbing the rest of the impact. Shattered beyond repair, the neoprene case was the only thing holding it together.

Setting the now-useless phone aside, Connor inspected his arm. A thin stream of blood ran down from a gash where the first bullet had nicked him, but the fabric had been strong enough to deflect the round and protect him from more serious injury. He cautiously flexed his arm, making sure he could still move it.

"Halkan imoow."

Connor looked up, the fog in his head instantly clearing as his senses were brought into sharp relief by the booming voice. The pirates. He could hear the soft pad of their bare feet on the deck above.

Connor scrambled away from the stairs. But no one descended to look for him. Risking a glance up, Connor crept back to the foot of the staircase. A pirate was standing over Cali, speaking rapidly in his mother tongue. Cali replied. The pirate nodded, seemingly satisfied.

"I soo raac," he said, striding up the stairs to the upper deck and beckoning Cali to follow.

As Connor watched Cali obediently go with the man, he clenched his fists in silent fury. This supposed stowaway had delivered the *Orchid* straight into the pirates' clutches. But at least he knew the girls and the rest of the crew were safe within the citadel. Then Connor remembered what Brad had said: *The citadel is effective only if everyone makes it inside.*

That included himself, Connor realized with dread.

Another pirate entered the upper corridor, dragging two gas canisters toward the galley. Connor pulled back from the staircase, praying he hadn't been spotted. Then he heard more feet in the corridor.

This time they were heading his way.

13

"I can't do this again," said Emily, her breathing becoming shallow and rapid. Her eyes anxiously scanned the confines of the cabin as if the walls were closing in on her. "I-I . . . can't survive again—"

"Will you shut up!" snapped Amanda, biting at one of her perfectly manicured nails. "You're making us all nervous. At least you've experienced this before. You know what to expect."

"How can you say that?" Chloe cried, drawing her trembling sister into her arms.

Emily's eyes regained focus and fixed Amanda with a cold, empty stare. "I'll tell you what you can expect, Amanda. Constant gnawing fear. Never knowing what tomorrow, or even the next hour, might bring. Your hopes raised, then dashed. Again and again. Until your spirit is crushed. No comfort. You'll cry your eyes dry. You certainly won't get to wash your hair—"

"Be quiet, you jinx!"

"Jinx?" questioned Chloe, frowning.

Amanda nodded. "You have to admit your sister attracts bad luck. Taken hostage twice in two years."

Chloe narrowed her eyes at Amanda. "Funny you came on the scene about the same time," she shot back. "Perhaps you're the jinx!"

"Stop that sort of talk right now," interrupted Captain Locke. "We're all on edge. The key to surviving this is sticking together." He looked from the girls to Amanda and back. There was a grudging acknowledgment from the three of them. "We're safe as long as we're in here. The pirates can't touch us. And rescue will be on its way."

He glanced out of the porthole. But the horizon remained empty of hope.

"What's that noise?" asked Sophie, her eyes puffy from crying.

A harsh spitting sound, like water hitting hot oil, could be heard coming from the stairwell. Captain Locke and the chief officer exchanged an uneasy glance.

"I'll investigate," said the captain.

Cautiously ascending the staircase, he approached the steel bulkhead. At first glance all looked secure. Then he spotted the orange drip of molten steel trickling from the doorframe.

He called down for his engineer. Geoff bounded up the

steps and stopped dead by his side when he saw the white-hot line worming its way millimeter by millimeter along the frame.

"That's not good," he muttered.

"How long have we got?" asked the captain.

Geoff rubbed a hand across his haggard face and sighed. "Five hours, maybe less."

14

There was nowhere to hide in any of the bedrooms. The built-in closets were the first place the pirates would look. Connor thought about locking himself in the shower room in his cabin, but the doors were flimsy. One hard kick and the pirates would be onto him.

As he hunted for a suitable refuge, Connor spotted his go-bag in the corner of his bedroom. He snatched it up, the liquid body-armor panel being his only defense against AK-47 rounds. He just wished the bag itself wasn't luminous yellow—it made him a blindingly obvious target.

The voices of the pirates were getting closer. He could hear them ransacking the girls' bedrooms just down the corridor, laughing and shouting as they did so.

Checking to make sure the corridor was clear, Connor raced along to the tender garage. Hurriedly he opened the bulkhead door, slipped inside and closed it behind him.

The garage was almost peaceful, the noise of the maraud-ing pirates dampened by the door. Connor looked around in desperation for a place to hide. The locker room . . . the shower cubicle . . . the tender . . .

He supposed he could launch the tender—or even the Jet Ski—and make his escape. However, he doubted whether the tender or Jet Ski, as fast as they were, could outrun a turbo-charged skiff. And, even if he could escape, the Jet Ski's fuel tank would more than likely run dry before he reached help or dry land. But more importantly, as a guardian, the idea of leaving his Principals at the mercy of the pirates was unthinkable.

Behind him, he heard the bulkhead's lock rattle and saw the handle turning.

Panicking, Connor opened one of the storage lockers. It was full of wet suits. He was about to climb in and conceal himself when he noticed the small hatch in the deck. Of course, the bilge!

Connor twisted and yanked at the small recessed clasp. The hatch lifted to reveal a dark, unwelcoming hole. He could hear the slop of water and caught a whiff of acrid fumes. But with no time to reconsider, Connor stuffed his bag into the black hole, then clambered in after it. He pulled the hatch down over his head, clipping it into place—sealing the hatch and all light out.

15

Connor listened to the pirates as they tramped into the garage. The men were jabbering away, loud and fierce. Locker doors were banging open, and the tender rocked noisily on its mounting as someone leaped into the cockpit. A pirate passed directly overhead, the hatch cover creaking under his weight. Connor held his breath, not only against the noxious fumes in the bilge but from the fear of being discovered.

The shower was switched on, the running water sounding like rain. One of the pirates said something, and the others laughed. Then the slap of feet retreated across the deck and the voices faded away; Connor, however, didn't hear the bulkhead door being closed.

He waited a moment longer, heard no one, and let out a deep sigh of relief . . . before gagging on the foul air. A caustic mix of diesel, urine and worse assaulted his nostrils, and Connor was forced to breathe through his mouth, which made it just bearable.

Water, warm and slimy, slopped around his bare knees, and something firm bumped against his thigh.

Finding the absolute darkness unnerving, Connor remembered his sunglasses in the pocket of his shorts. Sliding them on, he flicked on the night-vision mode and the bilge was revealed in a pale, ghostly light. Barely more than a six-by-ten-foot steel box, the compartment pressed in on him like a polluted coffin. With the low ceiling forcing him to hunch over, Connor felt a sudden and overwhelming urge to escape its cloying confines. But he didn't have the option of leaving his refuge—not yet, anyway. Above him, the shower water was still running and a man was singing to himself. Connor could scarcely believe it. One of the pirates was taking a shower!

Gazing down at the filthy bilge water surrounding him, Connor realized he was very much in need of one himself. But that was the least of his concerns. He was trapped in the bilge, in a yacht hundreds of miles from the nearest help, pirates were swarming all over the boat and his Principals were in real danger of being taken hostage, or worse. A crippling sense of despair washed over him as he realized he'd utterly failed in his duty as a guardian. He felt as though he were somehow to blame for these disastrous events, even for Brad's death.

Suddenly grief welled up in Connor and he was overcome with tears. Although he'd seen an agent killed during his first assignment, he'd never witnessed someone dying at such close quarters, and certainly not a friend murdered in cold blood. Connor wondered if that was how his father had died, cut down in a hail of bullets while protecting the US ambassador. Swift, brutal and agonizing.

Connor recalled the words the priest had said at his father's funeral: *Do not mourn the man who died; rather be thankful that such a man lived.*

Connor tried once more to gain comfort from this. As he wiped away the tears with the back of his hand, his feet slipped from under him and he reached out for support. His hand found a steel strut, and he managed to steady himself. Glad to have avoided a dunking in the foul water, Connor looked around the bilge. He noticed a crumpled bottle of water and a litter of empty plastic wrappers on a ledge that ran the length of the compartment. This was Cali's hideout, of course. Cali the stowaway: the one responsible for signaling the pirates, the one really to blame for their predicament.

Connor felt his despair and grief disappear beneath a rising tide of anger, bringing focus and clarity to his thoughts.

He had to keep a grip on himself if he was going to survive. *Everyone else is safe in the citadel,* he reminded himself. They had access to food, water and the radio. Rescue would be on its way.

For him, it was simply a matter of staying hidden and holding out.

16

"Emergency over," announced Amir, leaning back in his chair. "The *Orchid*'s distress signal has been canceled."

"What . . . again?" Charley questioned, zooming over to his console.

Amir shrugged. "The EPIRB unit's stopped transmitting."

"Could it have just lost contact with the satellite?" Marc asked.

"No, I've checked that," said Amir. "There've been two satellite sweeps and no signal."

"Then we need an official confirmation," said Colonel Black, picking up the phone and dialing the Seychelles coast guard.

"Good morning, this is Colonel Black. You spoke with my colleague earlier regarding the motor yacht *Orchid*. What's the status on the vessel's most recent distress call?" The colonel listened intently. "Thank you," he said, a pensive expression on his face, and put down the phone.

"The coast guard received a satellite call from the *Orchid* confirming cancellation. The other yacht is out of danger too. So they've called off the search-and-rescue team."

"But this is the *Orchid*'s second distress call," said Charley. "This doesn't feel right to me."

Bugsy coughed into his fist for attention. "It's not uncommon for an EPIRB to trigger a false alert," he explained, chewing rapidly on a stick of gum. "The sensor can get wet or the unit knocked from its bracket. Maybe that's what happened when they were helping the other boat."

Charley looked to the colonel. "Was there any mention of the casualty?"

"What casualty?" asked Ling, walking through the door with Jody and dumping her bags, the flight labels still attached.

"The *Orchid*'s been attacked by pirates," said Jason, going over to greet her. "One of the crew was shot during their escape."

"WHAT?" exclaimed Ling, her eyes widening in disbelief. "I leave Connor for one day and this is what happens. I miss out on all the action."

"This is not the sort of action we want," Colonel Black said. He turned back to Charley. "No, there wasn't any reference to the casualty. But, unless there's been a serious change in his condition, there'd be no real need. However, I agree, two distress calls in a morning is troubling. Bugsy, call the *Orchid*'s satellite phone and speak directly to Captain Locke. Marc, get in touch with Luciana—see if she's had any communication since her arrival in the Maldives. Amir, contact Connor. Let's obtain positive confirmation ourselves before standing down."

The colonel addressed Ling. "Before you left the *Orchid*, was there any indication of problems with the yacht's comms systems?"

Ling shook her head. "Not as far as I know."

Alpha team waited in tense silence as Bugsy dialed the satellite phone, Marc called Luciana's cell phone and Amir launched his SOS app.

After his third attempt at connection, Bugsy announced, "The line's engaged, Colonel."

Colonel Black frowned. "That's potentially good news. It means they're communicating, at least."

"Not with Luciana," said Marc. "She's heard nothing."

"Tell her to remain on standby. Any response from Connor?"

Amir shook his head. "I've pinged him twice. Even sent a remote activation, but the SOS app isn't responding."

"Perhaps he forgot to charge his phone," suggested Richie.

"You're not helping," said Charley, giving him a hard stare. "We should inform the Seychelles coast guard."

Colonel Black shook his head. "Not yet. They won't relaunch a search-and-rescue just based on our concerns. Keep trying to contact the *Orchid* every fifteen minutes. If we don't get a response within the next hour, then we raise the alert."

17

Connor wondered how on earth Cali had spent a week hidden in the bilge. His eyes were already starting to sting, the skin on his legs itched and a headache was building. He'd pulled himself up onto the ledge. It was just wide enough for him to perch and keep his feet out of the water, but the steel beam was cold and hard, the rivets protruding into his backside.

Having retrieved his go-bag, grateful that Amir had designed it to be waterproof as well as buoyant, he took stock of his limited resources. Aside from Cali's half-empty bottle of water, he had four energy bars and a packet of glucose tablets. Cali's own little larder was bare, explaining the boy's need to raid the *Orchid*'s galley. If the hijacking went on for any length of time, Connor realized he would be forced to do the same.

He rummaged through the go-bag, careful not to drop anything, and found the med kit. Taking out an antiseptic wipe, he cleaned the wound on his arm, then covered it with a self-adhesive dressing. He took a couple of ibuprofen tablets to numb the pain. Then, with great difficulty on the narrow ledge, he changed his damaged polo shirt for a new T-shirt and a long-sleeved sweater. The double layer wasn't ideal, considering the bilge's airless and clammy atmosphere, but the discomfort was worth it for the increased bulletproof protection.

As he sorted through the rest of the go-bag's contents, Connor thought about triggering the SART in the pack's side. Then he recalled that the transponder had only a five-mile range and an eight-hour life span. If he was going to use it, he had to be sure it would be effective. The SART was now his only means of raising an alert. With his smartphone destroyed, he couldn't send an SOS message to Guardian HQ. And, until he could reach a radio, he was cut off from any backup support.

The most useful item in his possession, besides the night-vision glasses, was the Dazzler flashlight. At least he would have light. And a defensive weapon. He switched it on, the compartment flooding with light from its bright beam.

His situation didn't look any more promising in the light. Somehow the bilge seemed smaller and more confining. The realization that he was trapped in a steel box hit home. And every minute he stayed hidden in Cali's old refuge, he ran the risk of being discovered. Even if the pirates didn't yet know about this hideaway, Cali would surely tell them. Unless, by some miraculous chance, the pirates had forgotten about him in the confusion of the attack. But that wasn't a gamble Connor was willing to take.

As his beam swept the bilge, he spotted a service hatch just above the waterline. Dropping from his perch, Connor bent down to inspect. The lock was stiff, but by throwing all his weight behind it, he managed to open it. On the other side was another bilge compartment, bigger than his, and judging by how far it went back, this one appeared to be beneath the yacht's twin engines. Connor swung his flashlight beam around, revealing a hatch in the ceiling. Perhaps there was a way to evade the pirates after all.

18

"You said rescue was on its way," cried Amanda. "Then where is it?"

Her perfect blue eyes stared accusingly at Captain Locke while the rest of the crew looked to him for leadership and reassurance. Emily and Chloe sat numb and silent at the dining table, their two plates of rice and boiled fish barely touched and now stone cold.

"I don't know. I honestly don't know," admitted the captain, peering through the small porthole and seeing only empty ocean. "But it can't be far off," he added with false hope.

From the stairwell, the spitting hiss of the blowtorch grew louder with each passing minute.

"Shouldn't we arm ourselves?" said Scott.

"With what?" asked Chief Officer Fielding.

"Kitchen knives, flares, anything."

"No," overruled Captain Locke. "If the pirates breach the

bulkhead, fighting will be futile. It'll only result in more bloodshed."

"Are you suggesting we simply surrender?" said Amanda.

The captain offered a resigned shrug. "We're left with little other choice."

The pirates' angry voices now invaded their supposedly impregnable citadel. There was a huge clang as the door fell to the floor, followed by an unnerving silence. Everyone's gaze turned toward the forbidding stairwell.

Chloe clutched onto her sister as the soft pad of bare feet was heard descending the stairs. The dark muzzle of an AK-47 appeared first, followed by the jug-eared pirate. His eyes, bulging and bloodshot, flicked around the room while his finger twitched nervously on the assault rifle's trigger.

"Gacmaha madaxa saara," he barked, jerking the gun's barrel toward the ceiling.

Guessing the pirate's meaning, Captain Locke raised his hands obediently and the rest of the crew followed suit. Three more armed pirates descended the stairwell, quickly surrounding the hostages. One searched the crew's quarters and dragged out a groaning and pale Jordan, dumping him on the floor at their feet.

"Dhaqaaq!" said Juggs.

Captain Locke furrowed his brow. "I don't understand."

"Move," the pirate repeated in English, gesturing with his AK-47 to the stairwell.

Captain Locke looked to his crew and the girls, trying to maintain an air of calm authority. "Do as he says. The pirates won't harm us. They need us alive for the ransom nego—"

The butt of the AK-47 collided with the captain's jaw, splitting his lip. Blood sprayed across the dining table. Emily flinched away and Chloe let out a shocked yelp.

"No speak!" said Juggs, shoving the stunned captain toward the stairwell.

19

"Here, for your face," said Spearhead, offering the captain a cloth napkin from the salon's dining table. "Sorry—my men can be overzealous at times."

Warily accepting the napkin, the captain dabbed painfully at his swollen, bleeding lip. Then he straightened himself to his full height, which by no means could match the towering pirate. "I'm Captain Thomas Locke, in charge of the *Orchid* and responsible for this crew and guests. And you are?"

"Spearhead," he replied, thumping his chest with a clenched fist. "And I'm now in charge."

He took the captain's hat and placed it on his own head.

Powerless to do anything about the theft of his hat, Captain Locke said, "You do realize a search-and-rescue team is on its way. But if you leave now, you can escape punishment—"

Spearhead let out a booming laugh. "I think you're mistaken, my friend. No one is looking for you."

The pirate surveyed his hostages, who huddled on the cluster of white leather sofas under the watchful guard of his gang. The news of their hopeless situation hit them hard. Sophie began to weep. Kieran buried his face in his hands. Chloe started sobbing in her sister's arms, and Emily turned pale and started to tremble.

Spearhead frowned. "Where's the boy?"

"Do you mean the stowaway?" Captain Locke replied, jutting his chin in Cali's direction. Cali was in the corner with an older bucktoothed lad, armed with a revolver.

"Not him. I mean the white boy," said Spearhead.

"Connor's dead," cried Chloe, daring to look the pirate in the face, her tearful eyes flashing with anger.

Unmoved by her fury, Spearhead raised an inquiring eyebrow at Cali. "Is this true?"

Glancing over, Cali gave a single nod and pointed at Juggs. "He shot him."

Spearhead glared at the accused pirate. Juggs mumbled something, and Spearhead snorted. "No matter. The boy was of little value to us. Whereas you two"—he turned to Emily and Chloe, baring his bone-white teeth in a leering grin—"are valuable property. Along with yourself, Ms. Ryder."

Spearhead's gaze raked over the model as Amanda's expression flipped from fear to shock. "How do you know my name?" she demanded.

Laughing, Spearhead advanced menacingly toward her and the girls. "There's a great deal I know about you, about Chloe and, of course, about you, Emily."

Geoff stepped into the pirate's path. "Leave them alone."

Spearhead eyed the engineer with disdain. "Oh, I have no intention of harming them. But I can't say the same for you."

Geoff stood his ground a brave moment longer, then reluctantly moved aside.

Amanda braced herself for the worst. The girls shrank back from the pirate as he crouched beside them.

"Don't worry, Emily," soothed Spearhead, brushing a calloused finger along her soft cheek. "If your father pays up, you'll be back home in no time."

Standing and addressing the captain, he ordered, "Set a course for Hobyo."

Captain Locke hesitated before replying, "But we don't have enough fuel to reach Somalia."

Spearhead's hand lashed out like a viper, his knuckles catching the captain hard across the jaw.

"Don't ever lie to me again," snarled Spearhead as Captain Locke reeled from the blow, his split lip gushing fresh blood. "I know for a fact that this yacht has a range of four thousand nautical miles. Start the engines, NOW!"

20

Connor's eardrums almost burst at the sudden roar of the *Orchid*'s twin diesel engines kicking to life above him. The bilge rumbled like thunder, and the stagnant water rippled with the yacht's vibrations. Covering his ears, Connor now understood why Cali hadn't ventured any farther than the first compartment. His bones rattled as the propellers began to turn and the yacht got under way.

But this was good news, he realized. The chief officer had said one would need a computing degree to pilot the *Orchid*. And, with the crew secure in the citadel, Connor very much doubted that any of the pirates had the necessary skills or knowledge. Which could mean only one thing: they'd been rescued!

Wading through the oil-slicked water to the far end of the compartment, Connor found the hatch in the ceiling. He pushed it open and popped his head out. The engine room was glaringly bright, noisy but empty. Clambering onto the metal decking, he felt sheer relief at escaping the bilge's dark, tight confines. Even the engine room's diesel-tinged air was a joy compared with the stench of the bilge, and his throbbing headache and nausea soon began to fade.

Having been cooped up for several hours, though, his limbs were stiff and sore. He shook some life back into them, then strode over to the bulkhead door. Shouldering his go-bag, he eased the door open and entered the service corridor.

No one was around as he made his way to the access door leading to the main stairwell and lower-deck bedrooms. He checked the girls' rooms first, discovering they were both empty and their personal belongings ransacked and scattered all over the floor.

At the foot of the stairs Connor paused, experiencing a strong sense of unease.

Where is everyone?

His bodyguard instincts urged him to remain cautious as he climbed up to the main deck.

From the direction of the salon, he could hear music playing. A thumping party beat. Connor smiled to himself. They were celebrating. He almost rushed in to join them when he heard an unfamiliar voice shout above the music, the words indistinguishable but definitely not English.

He froze to the spot. He'd misread the situation. The pirates were still in control.

The salon door suddenly opened, and Connor dived into

Mr. Sterling's study, a little way down the corridor. A pair of pirates, jabbering away, passed right by, oblivious to him. Both of them had AK-47s slung across their backs. As they entered the galley, Connor caught a glimpse of the steel door to the citadel. It lay on the floor like a discarded cardboard cutout. Next to it were two gas canisters and a blowtorch. In an instant he knew what had happened.

His thoughts went to Emily and Chloe. *Where are they? Are they hurt? Alive, even?*

Then he became aware of his own predicament. He had to get back into hiding, fast. If the pirates found him, there was no telling what they would do. And he'd be of no use to anyone if he was captured.

But first he had to locate the girls. Confirm they were still alive.

As the two pirates raided the galley for party supplies, Connor crept back into the corridor and across to the door leading to the outer deck. Through the porthole, stars gleamed in the night sky. At least he'd have the cover of darkness to move about in. Once again, though, Connor wished his go-bag wasn't bright yellow. Yet he couldn't leave it behind. He might need the protection of its liquid body-armor panel at any moment.

Out on deck, the breeze was cool and sharp, helping him focus his awareness. Keeping to the shadows, he listened for any pirates, but heard none approaching.

The salon's floor-to-ceiling windows were obscured, both a blessing and a curse. Although he wouldn't be seen, he was forced to go to the glazed bay doors at the far end to look for the girls. With the aid of his night-vision sunglasses, Connor made sure the route was clear, then headed toward the *Orchid*'s stern. As he passed the salon, the music pounding from within, the windows suddenly became transparent, and he was caught like a rabbit in headlights.

On the other side, the pirates were laughing, shouting and dancing. The *Orchid*'s crew, numb with shock, had huddled on the leather sofas as if marooned. Amanda was gyrating to the music amid the pirates. But by the look on her face, it wasn't out of choice. Then the windows went obscure again.

Connor dropped to the deck, praying he hadn't been spotted. The windows continued to flick between obscure and clear, a pirate inside finding the optical trick astonishing and hilarious at the same time as he repeatedly pressed the switch. By some stroke of luck, he'd been looking the other way and the darkness had concealed Connor from anyone else.

During the strobe-like flashes of the room, Connor continued to search for the girls. He saw Cali pouring a steady stream of drinks for the celebrating pirates. At first Connor couldn't believe how reckless the pirates were being—getting out of control and making themselves vulnerable. Then he noticed that four of the men, positioned strategically around the room, weren't joining in on the fun. They were keeping a watchful guard over their hostages, maintaining total control of the situation.

Eventually Connor spotted Emily and Chloe in the far corner of the room, separate from the rest of the group and overlooked by their own personal guard.

Connor despaired. *How can I, one lone boy, fight back against a gang of fully armed pirates?*

He might have trained as a bodyguard, but he wasn't a soldier like his father. He'd learned to protect, not kill. And these were bloodthirsty men. They'd already proved their willingness to go to any lengths to achieve their aims by murdering Brad in cold blood. Who knew what they had in store for the hostages next.

With dismay, Connor turned away from the scene, realizing he didn't have any hope of rescuing the girls single-handedly. Then he heard Charley's voice in his head: *Whether you think you can or think you can't, you're probably right.*

One look at the sheer terror and despair on Emily and Chloe's faces spurred Connor to act. He was their only hope. And, although the odds were stacked against him, it was his duty to protect the girls . . . no matter what it took.

21

Connor stabbed at the buttons on the radio in the crew's quarters. But it remained stubbornly silent, its screen disheartheningly blank. He'd noticed the front panel had been removed, but he had replaced it, hoping that by doing so the unit would become operational again. No such luck. The only other radio he knew of was on the bridge—along with the satellite phone—and the pirates were occupying that area.

Putting down the dead receiver, Connor reassessed his options. He'd planned to get in contact with the coast guard and update them on the *Orchid*'s situation and their location. But, with the citadel's radio broken, he feared there wasn't any search-and-rescue operation in progress at all.

Connor returned to the idea of using the tender to make an escape. He could load it with extra fuel and provisions and then, somehow, free Emily and Chloe and—of course, the tender! That had a VHF radio in the cockpit.

Realizing that, even if he did make contact, he might have to hold out for a while, Connor first hunted around the crew's quarters for food supplies and anything else that might prove useful. He filled his go-bag with cookies, dried fruit, cans of tuna fish and bottles of water. He also found a lighter, a penknife and a flare gun, complete with a spare set of flares. Then he crept back up the stairs to the main deck.

Passing through the galley, the place now littered with garbage thrown carelessly on the ground, Connor peeked into the main corridor. The music was still pumping loudly, but there were no pirates in sight. Then the salon's door burst open and the pirate with jug ears came staggering out. He lurched to one side, reached for the wall, missed and fell into an open cabin. Connor heard the pirate curse, struggle to his feet, then begin peeing into the toilet.

Seizing the opportunity, Connor dashed to the stairwell and down to the lower deck. He stopped short outside Chloe's room when he heard a rustling sound. A lone pirate was rifling through her belongings, pocketing any jewelry and valuables still left. While the thief was admiring a diamond ring that he'd discovered, Connor crept past toward the tender garage.

The door was still open. After a quick look inside, Connor entered, locked the door and hurried over to the tender. He clambered into the cockpit and located the radio and GPS unit. Switching them on, he was relieved to see a green light and their screens illuminate. Flipping up the safety cover on the radio, he pressed the red DSC Distress button and held it for five seconds, then waited for confirmation of a response.

Nothing registered on the screen.

Connor checked his watch as fifteen seconds went by, then thirty, without any response.

He picked up the handheld receiver, switched the radio to Channel 16 and pressed the Transmit button.

"Mayday, Mayday, Mayday," he said as loudly as he dared into the mic. "This is motor yacht *Orchid, Orchid, Orchid*. Mayday *Orchid*. Our position is"—he looked at the GPS unit and saw it was still searching for a satellite connection—"mid–Indian Ocean. We've been hijacked by pirates. We require immediate assistance. Over."

Releasing the Transmitter button, he prayed someone, anyone, would answer. But all he got was static.

He tried again. Nothing. And again.

Connor was about to give up when he noticed he'd forgotten to switch the radio to high power. Cursing his own haste, he sent out the Mayday call once more, now at full transmission power.

The radio crackled and hissed.

Then a voice burst from the speaker: "ORCHID . . . *MANGYARING ULITIN*."

The words echoed around the garage, and Connor

grabbed the radio's volume knob, twisting it virtually to zero in his panic.

"Orchid . . . *mangyaring ulitin,*" came the voice again.

Connor had no idea who the person was or what language was being spoken. It struck him that he could even be talking to one of the pirates. But that was a risk he'd have to take.

"This is Connor Reeves. I'm on board the *Orchid*. We've been hijacked by pirates. We need help urgently. Over."

The radio squelched and spat. "Orchid . . . *maaari kong . . . bahagya marinig mo . . .*"

The signal appeared to be getting weaker.

"I don't understand," Connor hissed desperately. "Do you speak English? Over."

The radio whistled amid a wash of static, the voice barely louder than a whisper.

"Hello?" persisted Connor. "Can you hear me—"

Behind him, the bulkhead door thunked as the lock disengaged. Cutting the power to the radio, Connor lay flat in the bottom of the tender. The door swung open on well-oiled hinges, and he heard the soft pad of bare feet enter.

"*Iska warran?*" said a man.

Connor stayed stock-still, not even daring to breathe. He sensed the pirate approaching the tender.

"*Iska warran?*" repeated the pirate, now less certain.

The pirate was no more than a couple of feet away from

him. Connor's eyes searched the bottom of the tender for a makeshift weapon. But everything was neatly stowed away. He could try to reach into his go-bag for either the Dazzler or the flare gun, but he feared any movement would alert the pirate to his presence.

After what seemed an age, the feet padded away and the bulkhead door closed.

Connor let out a long sigh of relief and lay there a moment recovering. Once convinced the pirate had gone, he sat back up and switched on the radio.

"Hello! Are you still there? This is motor yacht *Orchid*. Over."

The radio hissed steadily, but no one answered.

22

"I demand that the Seychelles coast guard launch a search-and-rescue mission now," Mr. Sterling shouted, his face flushed with anger on the videoconference screen.

"I've tried, but after two false alerts they're understandably reluctant to expend their resources on a wild-goose chase," Colonel Black explained, keeping his tone even as he sat behind the mahogany desk in his office. "Furthermore, both distress calls have been canceled by the *Orchid* herself."

"But no one can get through to them. We don't know what's happened. They could be shipwrecked or lying dead at the bottom of the sea. It's been over six hours. Surely the *Orchid* should be reported missing!"

"We're in agreement on that. I've been speaking with my military contacts to establish if there's a navy vessel in the area—"

There was a knock at the door, and Charley poked her head through.

"Sorry for interrupting, but Amir's just intercepted a Mayday relay."

"Hold on, Mr. Sterling, we may have some news."

Charley wheeled herself over and presented the colonel with a printout:

```
    Filipino fishing boat reported Mayday
call at 2014 hours local time. Message
garbled. Bad signal. Transcript of
call: "Mayday . . . day . . . This
is . . . Orc . . . Orchid . . . Our
position is . . . require immediate
assistance . . . Conn . . . eves . . .
need help . . . Do you . . . speak
Engl . . . Can—"[END]
```

"What's the news? Are my girls okay?" Mr. Sterling inquired as Colonel Black read the transcript.

Charley looked up at the screen. "There's very little information, I'm afraid, Mr. Sterling. Only that the Mayday was made from the *Orchid*, apparently by Connor."

On the monitor Mr. Sterling frowned. "Why's he sending the Mayday? Why not the captain or the chief officer?"

"Perhaps they can't," Colonel Black replied, putting down the transcript. "Just be glad it was Connor. At least we know he's alive. Which means your daughters are still under his protection."

Mr. Sterling grunted. "What can he possibly do if they're all in trouble?"

"I assure you, Mr. Sterling, Connor will do everything in his power to keep them safe." The colonel glanced at Charley. "Do we have the *Orchid*'s position?"

Charley shook her head. "No, but the fishing boat was fifty-six nautical miles east of her last known location. The distress call was sent by VHF radio, so the *Orchid* would have been within a ten-nautical-mile range of that."

"What's being done to find them?" asked an irate Mr. Sterling.

Charley replied, "A French frigate, the *Victoire*, has altered course to begin the search."

The colonel raised an eyebrow. "I know that ship. A unit of Royal Marines was posted aboard as part of a joint operations treaty between the United Kingdom and France. I should be able to get a direct line of communication with their commander."

"Good. I'm paying top dollar for your services, so I expect results," snapped Mr. Sterling.

"We have to be realistic with respect to our chances of finding them," said Colonel Black. "The fact that it's night will hamper operations, and it's one ship searching a large area of ocean. However, such frigates are equipped with advanced radar, sonar and infrared detection equipment. They've also got a starting coordinate to work from. This all works in our favor."

Mr. Sterling nodded. "Then inform me as soon as the *Orchid* is located. I want my Amanda and the girls back safe and sound." He cut the call, and the conference monitor went blank.

23

As dawn approached, Connor shifted position on the narrow ledge, trying to relieve the places where the steel rivets were digging into his backside and the cold was seeping into his bones. The bilge was a living hell to hide in, but at least he'd found some earplugs in the engine room, making his hiding place tolerable if not comfortable.

Sitting in the darkened bilge, spooning cold tuna into his mouth, Connor didn't miss the harsh irony of his situation. *He* was now the stowaway on board a hijacked ship.

Most of the pirates were sleeping late after the previous night's celebrations, and as a result, none of them had ventured down to the lower deck for the past few hours. However, acutely aware that he couldn't risk being discovered, Connor had stayed holed up below for the majority of the night.

Twice he'd made a trip to the upper decks to collect more provisions and pack the tender for a possible escape. The storage boxes under the seats were now crammed with food and water, but so far he'd managed to locate only a couple of emergency fuel cans.

Also, he'd continued trying the radio at half-hourly intervals, repeating the Mayday call and waiting in hope for an answer. None ever came, although once he thought he'd heard some garbled transmission.

His other problem was figuring out the *Orchid*'s position. The GPS in the tender failed to connect with the satellite every time, and Connor began to wonder if the yacht's hull was blocking the signal. The interference from the hull was probably also limiting the radio antenna's range, which would explain why he wasn't picking up any transmissions.

To counter this, Connor had considered opening the bay doors to the garage. However, he knew that would immediately bring the pirates running. So, using the screwdriver on his newly acquired penknife, he'd tried to remove the radio from the tender instead. But the radio was all wired in, and he feared any more tampering would break his only means of communication.

Connor looked at his watch—4:26 a.m. In one of his foraging missions, he'd come across a small compass and established that the *Orchid* was heading in a westerly direction, no doubt to Somalia. He was running out of time. If he didn't make contact soon, the *Orchid* would sail out of international waters and beyond all hope of help.

24

"We've had a breakthrough," Colonel Black announced as Charley, Amir and the rest of Alpha team entered the briefing room. "The *Orchid*'s EPIRB has been triggered again."

Despite it being 3:30 a.m. in Wales, the news quickly dispelled the bleary eyes and stifled yawns.

"This can't be another false alert," said Charley, speeding over to her monitor and scanning the report. "The *Orchid* must be at full throttle! She's gone some distance since Connor's Mayday."

"Don't worry," said the colonel. "The *Victoire* is already on course to intercept."

The phone in the briefing room rang, and Colonel Black picked it up. He listened intently for a moment. "Your help is greatly appreciated, Commander."

Placing a hand over the receiver, he addressed Alpha team. "The commander of 815 Squadron has arranged a live link to the operation. He's patching us through now."

Colonel Black switched to speakerphone, and Alpha team huddled around the desk to listen.

"*Victoire* to *Archangel*. You are cleared for takeoff . . ."

The Lynx helicopter rose from the deck of the *Victoire* and banked away into the early dawn sky. The ocean was a cold steel gray, the sun yet to grace it with its warmth. As the helicopter scudded low over the waves, the pilot and his observer scanned the horizon. Apart from a fishing trawler to the west, a large net dragging in its wake, the ocean was empty of shipping traffic. The pilot continued to head on the course dictated by the *Orchid*'s beacon.

In the cabin behind, two Royal Marine snipers perched either side, checking the sights on their long-range rifles in preparation for action. With hijacking a distinct probability, resistance was to be expected, if not wanted.

A blip sounded on the helicopter's radar.

"*Archangel* to *Victoire*," said the pilot. "Vessel located sixteen nautical miles due south."

Slightly adjusting course, the Lynx helicopter darted over the ocean.

"There!" said the observer, pointing straight ahead.

In the glow of first light, a yacht appeared on the horizon.

. . .

Alpha team listened in tense silence to the live relay. Static cut in and out, but the words were clear enough.

"*Archangel* to *Victoire*. Target in sight."

Amir smiled reassuringly at Charley. She responded with a flicker of a smile, then became tight-lipped again, her brow taut with concern.

"Target sailing on a northeasterly bearing. Speed, fifteen knots."

"At least they're not sinking," Marc commented.

"Yeah," said Ling, "but who's sailing her?"

It was a long time before the pilot spoke again, and tension in the briefing room rose another notch.

"Closing in on target . . . Snipers at the ready . . ."

"Do you think there'll be a firefight?" asked Richie, a little too eagerly.

"Shh!" said Charley, glaring at him.

"No sign of anyone on deck . . . Hang on . . ." Over the speaker the thud of the Lynx's rotor blades sounded like distant heavy gunfire. "I see someone . . . port side . . . a body . . . male . . ."

"Connor?" questioned Amir, saying out loud what was on everyone's minds.

Charley closed her eyes. "I pray it isn't," she whispered.

"But where's the crew?" asked Jason.

"If pirates have hijacked the *Orchid*, they'll hold all hostages below deck," Colonel Black explained. "Now be quiet."

"*Archangel* to *Victoire*," the pilot's voice said. "Reconfirm target's call sign."

"*Victoire* to *Archangel*. *Orchid*, I repeat, *Orchid*," replied the frigate's captain.

"Then we have a problem. EPIRB location confirmed, but name on hull is *Sunriser*, I repeat, *Sunriser*."

25

Mr. Wi-Fi's grin widened as he scanned the intercepted messages from the *Victoire* to the Seychelles coast guard on his laptop screen. Oracle's idea to plant the *Orchid*'s EPIRB beacon on the other yacht and remote-trigger it had worked like a dream. All the efforts of the search-and-rescue team were focused entirely on the wrong patch of ocean.

He glanced across at Oracle, who was reclining upon his bolster, picking at a bowl of fresh dates. The morning sun streamed through a barred window, suffusing the spacious living room in a golden light.

"They took the bait," he said.

Oracle replied with a smug smile as he popped a date into his mouth. "Of course they did. Dumb Westerners."

"With any luck, the *Orchid* should have a clear run."

"When can we expect our prize?"

Mr. Wi-Fi switched to the live tracking program on his laptop. "Around dawn tomorrow."

Reaching for the slim smartphone on the divan, Oracle pressed the Speed-Dial button.

"Then I better inform our investor."

26

Connor peered through the glazed doors at the far end of the salon. Dusk had settled, and once again he took advantage of the darkness. Several times he'd attempted to carry out surveillance during the day, but the pirates had been up on deck maintaining a constant watch for any approaching boats, which made it impossible for him to move about the yacht without being spotted. So he'd stayed below, biding his time for the right opportunity to attempt a rescue.

The once pristine and stylish salon was now a mess in the aftermath of the pirates' party. Empty bottles and broken glass littered the floor. Discarded food stained the white leather sofas, armchairs and carpet. The hostages appeared dazed, zoned out from a combination of gnawing fear and sheer exhaustion. The crew, minus the captain and the chief officer, remained under armed guard, the pirates lazily pointing their AK-47s in their direction while chatting with one another.

Chloe and Emily were still sitting apart from the rest of

the group. They huddled together in an armchair, Chloe dozing fitfully while Emily stared into space. Connor himself had barely slept for the past thirty-six hours, the narrow bilge ledge not exactly being comfortable. Yet, despite his frayed nerves, he'd managed to get some rest, knowing that sleep deprivation would cloud his judgment and that he had to stay sharp if he was to succeed in his mission.

As he shook off his weariness, Connor wondered how he could attract the girls' attention without being noticed by the pirates. He had to communicate his plan to the twins. Connor knew his best chance of success lay in completely separating them from the rest of the group. Then he'd have to deal with only one armed guard.

But neither of the girls was looking his way. Tapping on the glass would draw everyone's attention to him, so he'd have to come up with a better plan . . .

Without warning, a hand seized Connor by the shoulder and wrenched him to his feet. A gangly pirate with a hooked nose and wispy beard was glaring at him with furious astonishment.

"I soo rac!" he ordered, dragging him toward the doors.

Connor made a split-second decision. He could either surrender or . . .

Flicking his hand out like a snake, he hit the pirate in the throat with a knife-hand strike. Choking, unable to breathe or cry out, his eyes bulging, the pirate staggered backward under the blow. But he proved stronger than he looked and somehow managed to keep a grip on Connor. He swung a bony fist into Connor's gut. Connor tried to absorb the blow, but it struck hard. All the air was forced from his lungs, and he doubled up in agony, slumping to his knees. The pirate slugged him in the jaw, and stars exploded across Connor's vision.

However, Connor had taken punches just as hard many times before. During his years of kickboxing training, his body had become accustomed to the sudden shock of a punch or kick. His adrenaline masking the pain, he quickly got back on his feet.

Twisting himself in the man's grip, he clasped the pirate's fingers and rotated them against their joints in a jujitsu locking technique. The pirate grimaced and let go. Connor side kicked him in the ribs with all his might. A bone cracked. Wheezing, the pirate collided against the access gate in the stern's handrail, the gate gave way and he tumbled over the side.

Connor rushed to the rail, but the pirate had already disappeared beneath the dark swell of the ocean, the *Orchid* powering on into the night.

Panting and in pain, Connor dropped to his knees and tried to recover his breath. But almost immediately he heard voices heading his way. Dragging himself over to the stairs, he staggered down to the lower deck and dashed for the refuge of the bilge.

27

"You should prepare yourself for the worst," said Colonel Black, addressing the conference screen in his office.

Mr. Sterling's expression hardened, the lines around his eyes deepening.

"All evidence indicates that the *Orchid* has been hijacked by pirates."

Mr. Sterling nodded gravely, the blow heavy but inevitable. "And what about my family?"

Colonel Black leaned forward on his desk, his fingers interlaced. "No news yet. But it's likely they've been taken hostage."

"What makes you believe they're still alive? The entire Dutch crew was murdered."

"The *Sunriser* was hijacked so she could be used initially as a mother ship, then, with the false Mayday, as a deception to draw the *Orchid* into their net. Finally, by planting the EPIRB, she was a decoy to keep search-and-rescue off the scent. However, once the *Sunriser* and her crew had fulfilled their purpose, they were expendable. Your family is not. Considering the calculating nature of this hijack, I suspect the *Orchid* was specifically targeted."

Mr. Sterling sat up, his face filling the screen. "By whom?"

Colonel Black held up his hands. "Too early to tell. But this isn't standard operating procedure for Somali pirates. We'll just have to wait for them to contact us and deliver their ransom demands. Then we may find out more—"

Mr. Sterling thumped his desk, causing the webcam image to flicker. "I'm not going to sit here and do nothing while my Amanda, and my daughters, are at their mercy! I intend to fly out to the Seychelles tonight."

"But Mr. Sterling, any negotiations could take weeks to—"

"Don't argue with me. I want you on-site too."

"Absolutely," replied Colonel Black, his concern for Connor at the back of his mind. "We'll shift operations to the Seychelles Regional Anti-Piracy Coordination Center at once. I also have an expert ransom negotiator I can recommend."

Mr. Sterling shook his head. "No, I'll be doing the negotiating."

"But, Mr. Sterling, with the greatest respect, you're emotionally involved in this."

On-screen, Mr. Sterling jabbed a finger at Colonel Black.

"I didn't get this far in business by being emotionally involved. I've brokered multibillion-dollar deals before. This is no different."

"This is your family we're talking about. Not some company or asset."

"Exactly. So I'm not trusting the negotiations to anyone else. I freed my daughter last time. I'll free my family this time. On my terms."

Yes, but at what cost to your family? thought Colonel Black.

28

The heavy rumble of the engines eased, and Connor sensed the yacht slowing down. Opening his eyes, he glanced at his watch in the darkness—6:36 a.m. Somehow he'd managed to snatch a few hours' sleep, but he still felt groggy and nauseated. His jaw ached and his stomach muscles were tender. The shock of the hijacking, the exertions of the fight and the need for constant alertness were all beginning to take their toll.

A ghostly vision of the pirate's startled face as he toppled over the stern swam before Connor's eyes. A sense of guilt about the man's fate was hanging like a heavy chain around his neck. But Connor reminded himself that he had no way of knowing that the gate would open. And, under the circumstances, was he really to blame? He'd been fighting for his freedom and that of the girls.

Thankfully, after he'd escaped to the bilge, no one had come searching for him. Either the pirates didn't yet realize their comrade was missing or they'd presumed he'd fallen overboard. Whatever the reason, Connor knew he'd had a lucky escape. But he couldn't afford to make such a mistake again.

Cautiously, he emerged from the bilge into the engine room—as ever, glad to leave the suffocating coffin-like box. Making his way to the lower deck, he heard shouts coming from the stairwell. A man was barking commands and feet thumped overhead, followed by the noise of urgent activity.

Connor crept past the stairs toward his former bedroom. Ignoring the mess the pirates had made, he peeked out through a porthole. The morning sun was crawling above the horizon, a shimmering orange ball like the eye of a waking giant. At the far corner of his vision, he spied a barren coastline still shrouded in darkness. Dotting its countless inlets were the silhouettes of several large container ships. They lay motionless in the water like floating bloated bodies in a graveyard of forgotten ships. Connor swallowed hard, feeling that the noose had tightened around their necks.

Then a huge shadow was cast over the *Orchid* as a massive tanker loomed into view. Its blue and rusting hull rose sheer from the sea to its main deck high above. From Connor's limited view of its stern, the tanker appeared endless, its hull disappearing beyond his vision.

The *Orchid* was on a direct collision course and showed no sign of stopping.

Connor braced himself. Although the yacht was going no more than a few knots, the impact was still shocking. The *Orchid* shuddered from stem to stern, there was a screeching of metal and a loud *clang* echoed through the tanker's hull. As the *Orchid* rebounded off the hull, Connor caught a glimpse of a gangway being lowered from the tanker's main deck to the yacht's stern. Then he heard the *Orchid*'s anchor being dropped.

Whether they liked it or not, they had arrived in Somalia.

29

"Move!" ordered Spearhead, jabbing his gun at the hostages.

Captain Locke led his shell-shocked crew up the steep gangway. With as much grace as she could muster, Amanda followed close behind with Chloe and Emily in tow, the sisters clasping each other's hands for moral support. Their feet tramped up the metal steps in a slow march of despair. Far below, between the grilles, the wash of the green-blue ocean could be seen lapping against the rusting hull, no longer so inviting for a swim.

Reaching the main deck, the hostages were greeted by yet more armed men. Once aboard the pirate stronghold, the last vestiges of hope drained from the hostages' faces.

The deck itself was vast. An industrial network of walkways, pipes and machinery lined its length and breadth. The domes of several large storage tanks could be seen, upon which yellow warning signs declared Contents Highly Flammable. The bow was so far away that it could have been part of another ship. At the stern, the navigation bridge towered over them like a skyscraper. Most bizarre was the sight of a pair of skinny goats tethered to the rail on the starboard side. They bleated indignantly at the new arrivals.

"Welcome to Somalia," said a man cheerily, stepping from the disorganized ranks of pirates. Better dressed than the others, the man wore a pressed olive-green shirt, a cotton *ma'awis* in a black diamond pattern and a bloodred shawl slung over his shoulder. His face was smooth and his nose wide, and his teeth were stained green from khat leaves, but he kept his eyes hidden behind a pair of silver-mirrored aviator sunglasses.

"It wasn't our preferred destination," answered Captain Locke.

The pirate laughed. "It's good that you retain your sense of humor, Captain. I'm Oracle."

He offered his hand in greeting. Captain Locke ignored it.

"Oh, come now, Captain. No need to be so impolite."

Captain Locke's cheeks flushed with anger. "You expect me to shake your hand after your men have hijacked my yacht, killed two of my crew and taken us hostage! I have an injured crew member in need of urgent medical attention. That's my immediate concern."

Oracle waved away his grievance, barely glancing in the direction of the pale and feverish Jordan. "With any luck, I won't need to detain you for long. Now please, follow me."

With several threatening prods from their guns, the pirates shepherded the group of hostages along the metal deck. Reaching the base of the tanker's bridge tower, Oracle led them through a hatch and down a narrow corridor to a large open stairwell.

"Captain, my men will take you and your crew to your new quarters," Oracle informed him. He barked an order in Somali. With a rough shove, Juggs and several other armed pirates hustled them down the steel stairs into the bowels of the tanker.

"Not you, ladies," said Oracle, addressing Amanda, Chloe and Emily. "You're my most precious cargo."

Captain Locke glanced anxiously back at the girls, sensing this might be the last time they would see one another. Then he was gone with the others.

"This way, if you please," said Oracle, heading up the stairs.

With Spearhead behind them, Amanda and the girls were left no choice. They followed Oracle up two flights and down a stark white corridor to a wooden door. Outside stood a pirate on guard duty. He opened the door at their approach, and Oracle strode into the cabin.

"Captain Takayama, you have guests," said Oracle. "Do make them feel welcome."

A stocky Japanese man with round metal-framed spectacles rose from his chair. He blinked in surprise at the appearance of a woman and two girls on his ship, then bowed a respectful greeting.

"Well, I'll leave you to get acquainted." Oracle smiled warmly at Emily and Chloe as if he were their long-lost uncle. "I'll be contacting your father for the ransom. If he cooperates, you'll be home sooner than you think."

"Good luck with that," Emily muttered under her breath.

Oracle raised an eyebrow at her. "Then perhaps we'll need to persuade him." He motioned to Spearhead. "Bring her with us."

The pirate seized Emily by the arm and dragged her toward the door.

"No!" cried Chloe, clinging tightly to her sister's hand.

Spearhead shoved her away and she crumpled to the floor.

"*Yamae!* Stop!" cried Captain Takayama, moving to intervene.

The guard leveled his gun at him and the captain backed away, his head bowed in submission.

Spearhead hauled Emily out, slamming the door shut behind them.

As Chloe sat sobbing on the floor, Captain Takayama glanced awkwardly at Amanda, waiting for her to comfort the girl. When she didn't make a move, he helped Chloe onto a threadbare sofa. "I'm Captain Takayama of the chemical tanker *Golden Phoenix*. My crew members are held below." He offered her his handkerchief. "I am very sorry that you've been captured by these thugs too."

"Thank you," said Chloe, wiping her eyes. "I'm sorry for you and your crew as well."

The captain nodded sadly, then said, "I'll make you both some tea."

As the captain busied himself, Amanda stared morosely out of the porthole. "How long have you been held here?" she asked.

Captain Takayama offered her a thin regretful smile. "Five months and thirteen days . . . so far."

30

With the satellite phone clamped to his ear, Connor crouched beside the comms unit on the *Orchid*'s bridge, listening to the repeating ringtone.

"Come on," he urged under his breath. "Pick up."

He'd finally managed to access the satellite phone, but now no one was answering.

After the hostages had been escorted off the *Orchid* at gunpoint, he'd waited for everything to quiet down before making his move. But his hopes of a deserted yacht were dashed when he discovered two pirates sprawled on the leather sofas in the salon. Fortunately, they appeared to be half-asleep, chewing on mouthfuls of green khat leaves. It had been an easy matter for Connor to sneak past and up to the bridge. But he was keenly aware that he wasn't alone on board, so kept his eyes and ears alert.

After three more rings, a voice answered. "Hello?"

"Charley! It's Connor."

"Connor?" gasped Charley. "Where are you?"

"On the *Orchid*. Close to the Somali coast, I think." He glanced at the GPS unit and continued. "Our exact location is North five degrees, twenty-one minutes, eighteen seconds; East forty-eight degrees, thirty-three minutes, thirty seconds. We were attacked by pirates. Brad's dead. The girls and the crew have been taken onto a tanker. You need to organize a rescue immediately."

There was a pause. "You're hundreds of miles from where anyone is looking."

"So redirect the SAR teams here."

He could hear someone talking to Charley in the background. Her voice came on the line again. "Connor, you're in Somali territorial waters now. Colonel Black says that means direct military intervention is out of the question."

"So we can't be rescued?" said Connor, incredulous.

"You will be," assured Charley. "But we have to wait for the pirates to contact us with their ransom demands, then—"

A jaunty ringtone sounded aboard the yacht, making Connor flinch. He heard a man answer.

"I have to go," Connor whispered, replacing the receiver and dashing for the opposite door.

He slipped through just as a large pirate strode onto the bridge. Connor pressed himself against the wall of the corridor and held his breath. Continuing to jabber on his phone, the pirate set aside his AK-47 and plonked himself down in the captain's chair. He had a big nose and a wide mouth that seemed filled with too many teeth, and he talked so loudly that he was almost shouting.

Connor eyed the assault rifle and weighed his chances of snatching the weapon before the pirate could. But he'd never fired such a gun in his life. Even if he did grab it first, by the time he'd found and released the safety catch, the pirate would have easily overpowered him.

The pirate swung his feet onto the console and settled back, showing no signs of leaving the comfort of the captain's chair anytime soon. Connor realized he couldn't stand in the corridor all day. So, with one final regretful glance at the satellite phone, he silently edged away from the door and headed down to the main deck.

At least Charley and the rest of Alpha team knew he was alive. Where he was. And, most significantly, that he wasn't being held captive.

But for how long? He was on his own. No rescue was coming. Although he could hold out hope of a successful ransom negotiation, the process could take months.

Connor very much doubted Emily would be able to endure another lengthy hostage experience. He also feared that he'd lose track of the girls if they were transferred across to the mainland. But most worrying was the violent and unpredictable nature of the pirates. This more than anything convinced him that he alone had to rescue the girls sooner rather than later.

Connor had already prepared himself for such a mission. He'd dressed in his darkest clothes and baseball hat, and replaced his shorts with cargo pants. Into the pockets, he'd packed his night-vision sunglasses, the Dazzler and the flare gun. With some black gaffer tape from the storeroom, he'd covered the neon yellow of the go-bag and emptied it of everything nonessential. He wanted to travel light and move as stealthily as possible.

It also gave him enough room to pack the last of Chef's special pirate exploding cocktails.

As he crouched at the bottom of the tanker's gangway, he briefly contemplated waiting until dark. But that was ten hours off, and anything could happen to the girls in that time.

31

Connor was stunned by the sheer scale of the tanker. The deck alone had to be the size of two soccer stadiums. *How on earth will I locate the girls, let alone get them to safety?* he wondered.

The bridge tower seemed to be the most logical place to start searching. But that in itself was as big as an apartment building. At the very top Connor thought he saw movement—a possible pirate lookout. He'd have to be careful. At least the tangle of pipework, for loading and offloading the tanker's chemicals, provided him with good cover.

Darting from the gangway to the shelter of a mechanical pump, Connor picked his way along the deck. At one point, it seemed his ears were playing tricks on him. He could hear bleating.

Then he spotted a couple of goats tied to the starboard rail.

More hostages, thought Connor grimly.

He was more than halfway when the sound of voices alerted him to danger. He ducked behind a cluster of oil drums. A few moments later, two pirates strode by, laughing, barely bothering to look around them. If they were on guard duty, they clearly weren't concerned about the possibility of an attack or a rescue attempt.

From his hiding place, Connor watched as they approached the goats. One of the pirates untethered a scrawny gray one and led it over to an area of open deck. With a twist of its head, he pinned the poor beast to the floor. Crouching beside it, the other pirate drew a long curved knife. With a practiced hand, he slit the goat's throat and began to saw through the sinew and tendons.

Connor had to look away as the goat's pained and desperate bleats faded to a final gargled breath. When he glanced back, the deck was slick with blood. Connor flashed back to Brad's death, the security officer's corpse still lying on the *Orchid*'s deck, untouched and unmourned. If the pirates could murder Brad in cold blood and slaughter a goat with such a lack of compassion, he dreaded to think how they'd treat their hostages—or him if he was caught.

While the two pirates finished butchering the goat, Connor managed to stay hidden by weaving through the maze of pipes and metalwork as he made his way to the bridge tower. With a quick check above, he sprinted across an exposed walkway and ducked through a hatch. Inside he paused for breath, the image of the bleeding goat still fresh in his mind. It impelled him to keep going.

A narrow corridor led to an open stairwell. *Up or down?* he thought.

He guessed the hostages would be held on the lower decks, secure and out of sight. Connor was about to descend when he heard Emily's voice cry from above, "Let go! You're hurting me."

32

"We know exactly where my family is, Clive. Send in your warship now," demanded Mr. Sterling, his hand almost strangling the phone's receiver as he spoke directly with the Australian prime minister. "What do you mean, international incident? I'll give you a domestic incident that'll end your career if you don't rescue them at once."

Mr. Sterling's face purpled as he listened to the prime minister's reply. "Well, that's a fat lot of help!" He slammed down the phone. "Bloody politicians."

He paced the briefing room of the Seychelles Regional Anti-Piracy Coordination Center like a caged tiger. Colonel Black sat on the opposite side of the conference table, Charley next to him. Both waited for Mr. Sterling to calm down. Then the colonel said, "What did your prime minister have to say?"

Mr. Sterling stopped pacing and pulled out a chair. "He'll

station HMAS *Melbourne* off the coast of Somalia—twelve nautical miles out. A pointless gesture. What use is it there? Why can't my government be like the Americans and act? A few Navy SEALs and this would be over in no time."

"If you're referring to the *Maersk Alabama* hijacking, that US rescue occurred in international waters," explained the colonel. "Unfortunately, your prime minister's hands are tied. The Australian Navy can't breach Somalia's territorial waters without creating a diplomatic crisis."

"We already have a crisis!"

"Yes, but once a ship is taken, it's very hard to rescue the crew and passengers without loss of life. Moreover, as soon as the pirates see the warship coming, they'll relocate the hostages. All they're interested in is the money. The lowest-risk method is to pay a ransom."

"Fine," relented Mr. Sterling, holding up his hands. "So why haven't the pirates contacted us yet?"

Colonel Black didn't have an answer for that one.

They sat in silence, the air-conditioning unit whirring in the background. Mr. Sterling's bodyguard, Dan, poured his boss a cup of coffee, then offered one to Colonel Black and Charley. Declining, Charley gazed through the glass into the center's operations room. A live satellite surveillance feed on a monitor displayed a magnified section of the Somali coastline. In the waters beyond the port of Hobyo, several large cargo ships could be seen. Each contained hostages—more than a hundred seamen in total, from every corner of the globe, all waiting desperately for the shipping companies to pay their ransom demand. The chemical tanker in the middle, the *Golden Phoenix*, was where they presumed Mr. Sterling's family and crew were being held. In her shadow, barely visible, was the white outline of the *Orchid*.

Was Connor still aboard? Charley clasped her phone in her hand, praying for another call from him. But an hour had passed, and they'd heard nothing. Perhaps Connor had been captured? Charley tried to push the dark thoughts to the back of her mind.

A cell phone rang, breaking the tension.

Charley's heart leaped with hope until she looked at her phone's display and discovered it wasn't hers.

Mr. Sterling pulled his phone from his pocket. For a second or two, he stared at the screen. The number displayed a country code of +252. Somalia. He thumbed the Answer button, putting it on speakerphone.

A smooth, lightly accented voice spoke. "Hello? Mr. Sterling?"

"Yes," he replied cautiously.

"My name is Mr. Ali. I work for a local charity group in Somalia. I've heard about your family's plight. I want to help negotiate their release."

33

Connor crept along the corridor. He'd followed the sound of Emily's struggle up three flights, then lost her.

Despite the overwhelming urge to run, he couldn't rush his search for Emily or her sister. A pirate could appear at any moment. There were countless cabins, storerooms, alcoves and stairways from which they could materialize; the bridge tower was like a rabbit warren. Yet the dangers of encountering a pirate were matched by the safety that all the nooks and crannies offered Connor as places to hide.

As he approached an open door, halfway along the corridor, he heard a man speaking in English.

"No, I'm not a pirate myself," assured the honeyed voice. "As I said, my name is Mr. Ali. I volunteered to help. I want to save your family and crew."

Connor slipped into a storeroom across the hall. Peering around the doorframe, he gained a narrow view of the scene. A potbellied man with a receding hairline and greasy skin sat at a Formica-top table. Sweat patches blotted his dark green shirt, which hung limply over a pair of long chino shorts, and on his feet were a pair of worn plastic sandals. He had a cell phone wedged between his ear and left shoulder while lighting up a self-rolled cigarette. Blowing out a puff of smoke, he said, "I understand your concern. I will do my utmost to help."

Another man sat opposite. Connor caught a glimpse of a pair of silver-mirrored sunglasses and a bloodred shawl, but most of Connor's view was blocked by the mountainous pirate who'd hijacked the *Orchid*. Beside him stood Emily, small and frail by comparison.

Connor simply wanted to dash in, snatch her and flee the ship. But he knew he'd have to wait for the right moment if he was to rescue both the sisters. Besides, he was intrigued by the presence of this Mr. Ali and the hope he offered.

"Yes, I am on board," said the potbellied man, tapping the ash from his burning cigarette onto the floor. He eyed Emily and smiled; a tooth was missing, and the others were tinged a sour yellow. "Yes, I have seen your family and the crew. They're all in good health . . . for the time being."

Despite Mr. Ali's amiable tone, his last words smacked of a veiled threat. Mr. Ali took another draw on his cigarette and casually blew smoke rings into the still air.

"The pirates are demanding one hundred million dollars."

34

"One hundred million dollars!" exclaimed Mr. Sterling, staring at his smartphone in disbelief. "That's an outrageous figure."

Colonel Black and Charley exchanged astonished looks. Such a ransom was unheard of. The demand was more than half the total payout for all Somali hostages the previous year.

"It's that or you'll never see your family again," said Mr. Ali.

"Don't threaten me," snapped Mr. Sterling.

"Please, you must understand, I'm just repeating what the pirates ask me to. I don't want your family or crew hurt any more than you do."

"Then tell your pirates that—"

Colonel Black shot Mr. Sterling a warning look. They'd discussed their negotiation strategy. A calm, levelheaded approach was necessary. Somali pirates were known to be clever, aggressive negotiators and quick to take advantage of any signs of weakness.

Mr. Sterling took a deep breath and composed himself. "That figure is too high. I can't possibly raise such an amount."

"Mr. Sterling, one hundred million dollars is barely ten percent of your estimated wealth. I'm sure you can afford it."

"Estimated," repeated Mr. Sterling emphatically. "Most of my wealth is tied up in companies."

"Then I'd advise you to start selling your companies."

"That'll take months. I'm sure your pirates would prefer a quick resolution to this. Why don't we agree on two million and be done with it?"

A weary sigh was heard over the line. "I will ask, but time is what the pirates have in abundance."

There was muffled noise as a hand covered the speaker at the other end. Charley thought she heard the sound of incredulous laughter. Mr. Ali came back on the phone.

"They refuse your offer. It's one hundred million dollars. Nothing less."

Mr. Sterling clenched his fist. "But what they're demanding is five times any previous ransom."

"This is simply business for the pirates, Mr. Sterling. You must understand: supply and demand. Fewer hijackings means less supply. Therefore the pirates demand more. And what price can you put on family? Besides, one hundred million is nothing compared with what countries like yours have stolen from Somalia."

Mr. Sterling frowned, confused by the sudden line of argument. "What are you talking about?"

"Foreign trawlers plundering all our fish stocks. Tankers illegally dumping toxic waste on our shores. Your newspapers must have covered the story at some point."

"I'm sure they have. But those offenses have nothing to do with me."

"That may be true," replied Mr. Ali, "but they have everything to do with why these men are pirates."

Mr. Sterling started to respond, but Colonel Black held up his hand to silence him. They were getting bogged down in irrelevant argument. He hurriedly wrote a message on a piece of paper and passed it across the table.

Mr. Sterling read the note, then said to Mr. Ali, "Before we negotiate further, we need proof of life."

35

Connor watched as Mr. Ali beckoned Emily to the phone.

"Your father wants to speak with you."

"Daddy?" said Emily, her voice fragile. "No . . . I haven't been hurt."

As she cradled the phone, Connor could see her face. Her eyes were sunken with exhaustion, and her complexion was fearfully pale.

"Yes, Chloe's fine too. Amanda is with her . . . No, the pirates haven't harmed her . . . No, you can't. I'm not with them."

Connor could see that Emily was barely holding it together. Her hands trembled as she held the phone to her ear.

"Brad was shot dead . . . No, I don't know about the rest of the crew. They were taken below . . . Are you going to pay the pirates?"

She listened a moment. Her body visibly crumpled with

the answer. Her knees giving way, she clutched at the table to steady herself.

"Please. Just pay! Don't leave me like you did last time. I can't face it. I'll . . ."

The pirate with silver-mirrored sunglasses stood up. He pulled a Browning handgun from his belt and pressed the barrel to Emily's temple. Connor tensed, wondering if he could cross the distance before the pirate pulled the trigger.

"D-D-Daddy, I have a gun to my head." Emily began to sob loudly. "Don't let them kill me! Just give them whatever they want. PLEASE—"

The pirate snatched the phone from her grasp.

"This is Oracle speaking. We're not playing games, Mr. Sterling," he said, his finger going to the trigger. "You've got your proof of life. Now pay up, or I'll give you proof of death."

With that he fired his gun.

36

The gun blast distorted the phone's speaker. There was a scream, and then the line went dead.

"NO!" cried Mr. Sterling. He jabbed at the touch screen, bringing up the last call and redialing.

The phone rang out, its tone distant and taunting.

He looked to Colonel Black, almost pleading. "They're not answering."

"Negotiation is about control," said the colonel. "The pirates won't answer. They want to cause you as much distress as possible."

Mr. Sterling angrily shook the phone at him. "They just shot my daughter!"

"That's highly unlikely. They'd not wish to lose their main bargaining chip."

"But you heard her scream."

"Wouldn't you if a gun went off by your head?" said Charley, equally shocked by the disturbing call.

Colonel Black met Mr. Sterling's eye. "The pirates are simply trying to intimidate you. They've clearly done their background research. They know exactly what you're worth. This suggests a highly organized gang—which means they'll have the resources for a long-term hostage situation."

Mr. Sterling slumped back in his chair and rubbed at the bridge of his nose. "This is a nightmare. I can't believe it's happening all over again. This negotiation is nothing like the previous one. Who pretends to shoot their hostage on the first call? These pirates are worse than animals."

"The tactics of kidnap gangs vary according to where they are and who they are," replied the colonel. "What works with the Corsican Mafia may backfire with an Iraqi militia or a Colombian bandit—and, in this case, Somali pirates. But one thing remains constant: mistakes can cost lives."

Mr. Sterling's eyes reddened with tears. "My precious Amanda. She's so vulnerable. I should never have left her."

Colonel Black studied Mr. Sterling. A shadow of his former self, he was no longer the mighty media mogul—merely a father and husband-to-be, despairing for his captive family. So much for his claim of not getting emotionally involved in the deal making. "I think it's time to bring in a professional negotiator," he suggested.

Mr. Sterling sighed heavily. "No, maybe I should just pay the pirates. If I sell all my shares, I might be able to raise the capital within a few weeks."

"If you give in too easily, the pirates will simply up the asking price."

"From a hundred million dollars?"

The colonel held up his hands. "So far, this gang has proved shrewd, calculating and ruthless. Not a good combination. Who knows what these men are capable of?"

"There's still Connor," piped up Charley.

Mr. Sterling gave a humorless laugh. "What can he do? One boy against a gang of cutthroat pirates."

37

The gunshot had sent Connor's adrenaline pumping. He'd almost bolted from his hiding place in an attempt to save Emily. But the pirate who called himself Oracle had fired upward instead, blasting a hole in the ceiling.

Emily stood cowering from shock, a hand clasped to her deafened ear. "What did you do that for?" she cried.

Oracle grinned at her as he passed the phone back to Mr. Ali. "To put pressure on your father to pay. That's what you want, isn't it?"

Mr. Ali's phone began to ring.

"That'll be him now."

Mr. Ali started to answer, but Oracle shook his head. "Let him sweat awhile."

Pocketing his phone, Mr. Ali laughed, his yellow teeth making a mockery of his smile. Connor realized that the man was no charity worker. He wasn't on the ship out of the goodness of his heart. He was just one of the pirates, pretending to be an impartial negotiator.

"I expect Mr. Sterling will come back with another low offer," said Mr. Ali, rolling a second cigarette. "What do you want me to say?"

Slipping the gun back into his belt, Oracle considered this a moment. "Tell him we'll kill one of the crew for every offer he makes below one hundred million. That should persuade him to take our demands seriously."

This was a game changer, Connor realized. He had to free the girls before they started killing hostages. Once the pirates went down that route, no one was safe from a bullet—least of all himself.

Connor heard hurried footsteps coming down the corridor. He retreated from the door as a young boy in shorts and a grimy T-shirt rushed by and into the cabin opposite. For a second, Connor thought it was Cali. But the boy was slightly taller and older, with buckteeth. A revolver, too big for him, was thrust into the back of his shorts. Connor was stunned—even the kid pirates had guns!

The lad yammered something in Somali. Oracle and Mr. Ali exchanged astonished looks.

"What's going on?" asked Emily as Mr. Ali rose from his chair and headed for the door with Oracle and Spearhead.

"Nothing to worry your pretty little head about," said Mr. Ali. "We just found out our investor's come on board."

38

Bucktooth was left behind to guard Emily. Connor realized this was his best opportunity to attempt a rescue—he could go head-to-head with just one pirate. Emily was perched on the chair next to the Formica-top table, picking numbly at a loose piece of veneer with her fingernail. Bucktooth leaned against the wall, eyeing her long blond hair and pale skin with fascination.

With the boy distracted by Emily's appearance, Connor crept across the corridor and into the cabin, planning to snatch the gun and subdue the young pirate. However, as he entered the room, Emily's eyes widened in amazement. She tried to hide her reaction, but the boy had already noticed. He spun around faster than a rattlesnake, whipping the revolver from his shorts.

Connor darted forward, slamming an open palm into Bucktooth's chest and striking the solar plexus. The boy gasped, doubling over in pain. But still he tried to point his gun at Connor and take a shot. Connor grabbed his wrist and slammed the weapon against the wall repeatedly. Bucktooth dropped the gun. Connor kicked it away, then drove his forearm across the boy's throat, pinning him to the wall in a choke.

"Don't make a sound," hissed Connor, putting a finger to his lips. "Do you understand?"

Gagging, his eyes wide with fear, the boy nodded.

Connor slowly released the pressure and stepped back.

Bucktooth took a desperate gulp of air, then shouted, "*I caawi!*"

Given no choice, Connor drove an uppercut into Bucktooth's jaw. His head rocked back, his eyes rolled in their sockets and the boy collapsed to the floor in a lifeless heap.

"Did you kill him?" whispered a stunned Emily.

Connor shook his head. He'd connected perfectly with the sweet spot on the boy's jaw, the impact causing his brain to shut down. Bucktooth would be out cold for a good few minutes. When he did regain consciousness, he'd have no memory of even being hit.

Emily ran over and wrapped her arms around Connor, sobbing. "I thought you were dead."

"Almost," replied Connor. "I'll explain another time."

He dragged the unconscious Bucktooth across the corridor to the storeroom and locked him in.

"Come on—we have to find your sister," said Connor,

taking Emily's hand and heading down the corridor. "Do you know where she is?"

Emily nodded. "In the captain's cabin with Amanda."

Emily directed Connor down two flights of stairs and along another corridor. Connor, taking the lead, kept a sharp eye out for pirates. But the bridge tower seemed deserted. Most of the pirates, he guessed, were either on deck or guarding the hostages below. They came to a bulkhead door with a small round window.

"In there," said Emily.

Connor peered through the glass. He couldn't see any pirates, but his view was limited. "Let me go first."

Opening the door, he cautiously stepped into the room. It was full of boxes.

"This can't be right," he said, turning to Emily.

But she was no longer with him. Behind him, the bulkhead door clanged shut. Connor ran to it and yanked on the handle. It wouldn't budge.

He looked through the window and saw Emily turning the lock. Sealing him in.

39

"This is all your fault, Colonel Black!" snapped Mr. Sterling, pointing an accusing finger at him. "I can't believe you persuaded me to hire teenagers to protect my family. How could you be so reckless? Your organization is irresponsible and ill conceived. When this is over, I'm going to expose Guardian for the dangerous frauds that you are."

Colonel Black rose from his chair, thunder in his eyes. "You're angry and upset, Mr. Sterling," he said evenly. "Perfectly natural reactions under the circumstances, but the blame lies squarely with the pirates."

Mr. Sterling started to reply, but Colonel Black cut him off. "Need I remind you, you also employed an experienced crew and a ship security officer. But that didn't stop a determined and ruthless enemy. Brad's now dead. And at your insistence, Ling was dismissed. Which means Connor is your daughters' last and only ring of defense. Don't rule him out."

The two men held each other's stares. Charley knew

Colonel Black wouldn't back down. She'd seen him deal with such tense situations before, with the client becoming hotheaded and irrational under pressure. Clients rarely praised the security team when a mission went smoothly and nothing happened. But they were quick to attribute blame when things went wrong, even if it was their own fault for ignoring security advice in the first place.

A phone rang. All eyes went to Mr. Sterling's smartphone on the table.

"Is it them?" asked Charley.

Mr. Sterling shook his head. "It's my lawyer."

He held the phone to his ear and listened, then cupped a hand over the receiver. "He says a freelance reporter has gotten wind of the hijacking and wants to speak with me."

Colonel Black grimaced. "In this situation, the last thing we need is the media involved."

"I am the media," reminded Mr. Sterling.

"Then control it. Smother the story for as long as you can."

Returning to the phone, Mr. Sterling muttered, "My rivals are going to have a field day."

While he spoke with his lawyer, trying to limit the damage, Charley leaned close to Colonel Black and whispered, "I'm worried about Connor. We still haven't heard from him."

"He can handle himself," said the colonel.

"Shouldn't we be doing more to help him?"

"What can we do? He's on his own out there."

Colonel Black caught the sting in Charley's eyes at his apparent indifference.

"Listen, I'm just as concerned as you. But I can't let such emotions cloud my judgment," he explained. "I'm sure Connor's managing the situation. When he does get in contact again, inform him of HMAS *Melbourne*'s location. Find out everything you can about the pirates, the ship, the hostages' location, anything that might prove helpful in a rescue attempt."

"I thought you said military intervention was out of the question."

"Until all other avenues have been exhausted, it officially is." His steel-gray eyes flicked toward Mr. Sterling. "But, if the negotiations continue to go south, a Special Forces raid might be the only option left . . . whatever the risk."

40

Connor sat on the cold steel floor, staring at the locked bulkhead. He'd kicked at the handle, hammered on the lock with his flashlight, and even thrown himself against the door. But it refused to budge. He'd searched for another way out, but the storage room had no other exits, not even a porthole.

His mind whirled in a fit of anger, shock and confusion. He still couldn't believe that Emily had locked him in the room. She hadn't done it under duress. She'd been alone as she'd calmly walked away. Then she'd met the pirate called Spearhead in the corridor and, by the looks of it, willingly surrendered to him.

Has something snapped inside Emily's head from the stress of being a hostage again? Or is her medication to blame?

During their operation briefing Charley had pointed out that Emily's anti-anxiety drugs could cause impaired thinking. That seemed the most logical explanation for her behavior. The other was unthinkable . . . that Emily was somehow in league with the pirates.

But why? What does she have to gain?

Connor tried to think if there were any clues. The *Orchid* had been sailing far from the danger zone. There shouldn't have been any pirates for over five hundred miles. So how had they found the yacht?

Despite Ling's warning, he recalled Emily still posting pictures and comments on Instagram whenever they departed or arrived at a new location. Could she have been secretly communicating with the pirates? Sending their coordinates via geo-tagging?

Then the morning of the attack when he'd seen the flashing light, had Emily been responsible rather than Cali? Was she signaling the pirates? Connor tried to picture her expression when he'd found her on deck. Emily had definitely appeared surprised, even shocked . . . or was it guilt?

And, if she was conspiring with the pirates, it would explain why she'd been so quick to defend Cali. *Are they working together?*

The radio in the citadel had been sabotaged. Was that Cali's doing? Or Emily's?

Yet none of this took away from the genuine fear in her eyes, or the heartfelt plea to her father to pay the ransom, or the relieved hug she had given Connor on her initial rescue.

The pirate leader had even put a gun to her head. If Emily was with them, why would he do that?

There were too many questions. Too many conflicting possibilities.

The only known facts were that Emily had led him into a trap. And that he was now a hostage.

41

"I never expected to meet you in person," said Oracle, settling into a chair opposite the investor. "Nor did I expect you to be white."

The investor stared hard at the pirate, adjusting the cuffs of his gray shirt and saying nothing.

Oracle shifted uneasily under his gaze. The cabin they sat in was hot and muggy, and the man's presence seemed to intensify the discomfort.

"Not that it's a problem, of course," Oracle added. "Can I offer you some water? Your journey must have been tiring."

The investor nodded. Oracle clicked his fingers and barked an order at Cali, who was standing obediently in the corner. Cali rushed over to an old fridge, pulled out a bottle of chilled water and handed it to the investor. The white man took a measured sip, then replaced the cap. Cali backed away, not taking his eyes off him. To Cali, he was like a desert scorpion upon a rock. The rock appeared safe enough, but anyone getting too close would be struck with a lethal sting.

Oracle, a man used to being in charge, found his investor's silence unnerving.

"So, what brings you here?" he demanded. "As I reported, we've successfully hijacked the *Orchid* and are now waiting for the ransom to be paid."

"And it won't be long before we receive good news on that account, I can assure you," added Mr. Ali, keen to impress. "The cracks are already beginning to show. We should close this deal within a week or so."

He grinned broadly at the investor, awaiting his praise.

The investor didn't smile back. "Change of plan. When the ransom is delivered, you're not to release his family."

"What?" exclaimed Oracle, taking off his sunglasses and frowning. "What am I supposed to do with them?"

"Hand them over to Seven Sabers."

Mr. Ali's mouth fell open in shock. "The terrorists? But they'll torture and kill them."

"And you won't?"

"That was just an empty threat to force the price up," explained Mr. Ali. "We're not religious extremists. We're businessmen."

"I never make empty threats," said the investor. "What's the point?"

"But, if we double-cross Mr. Sterling, my gang will get a bad reputation," argued Oracle. "That's not good for business. Shipping companies won't pay next time."

The investor snorted. "With a share of a hundred million dollars in your pockets, what do you care? And since when did pirates worry about their reputation?"

"We're not terrorists. We're simply making a living from the sea. And since other nations have stolen all our—"

"Don't justify your crimes with false moral arguments. You are pirates, blood and bone. That's why we selected you. The organization I represent wants to break Mr. Sterling's heart as well as his bank balance. He's come too close to the truth too many times for our liking. We need his mind occupied until we've tied up all the loose ends."

"And who exactly do you represent?" challenged Oracle.

The investor's icy stare fixed upon him. "Such questions can get a man killed."

Oracle felt his blood rise. His hand went to his gun. "Are you threatening me?"

The investor didn't blink. "No, it's just a fact."

With an effort, Oracle subdued his anger and relaxed his grip on the gun. The investor had, of course, funded this hijacking and delivered a golden catch virtually into his lap. If the ransom came through, he'd become one of the richest men in Somalia overnight. Why not play his little game?

Oracle offered a civil smile. "I just don't understand why you couldn't tell me this over the phone."

"Because I needed to commend my little spy."

The investor turned toward the door. Emily stood there, accompanied by Spearhead and Bucktooth, nursing his jaw.

"Hello, my little sparrow. You have done so well."

42

Connor searched frantically through the boxes in the storage room. There had to be something that could help him escape. But all he'd found so far were spare machinery parts, gaffer tape and other repair supplies. As he rifled through the last box, Connor heard the door behind him unlock.

"You were supposed to be dead," said Spearhead, his bulk filling the open doorway.

The pirate had the barrel of his AK-47 trained on Connor.

"Sorry to disappoint you," said Connor, backing away, his go-bag clasped to his chest.

Scowling, Spearhead cocked his head to one side. "One of my men, Abdul, is missing. Was that your doing?"

Connor could only presume he meant the pirate with the hooked nose. "He fell overboard."

Spearhead narrowed his eyes. "Maybe you will too."

His finger went to the trigger. Connor braced himself for

the shot, the panel of liquid body armor suddenly feeling far too small a shield. From behind its limited protection, he reached for the flare gun in his pocket.

"Stop! What do you think you're doing, Spearhead?" said a voice from the corridor.

"About to shoot a ship's rat," replied the pirate.

Oracle appeared in the doorway and placed a hand on Spearhead's rifle, forcing the barrel to the ground. "All in good time, my friend, all in good time."

The pirate leader stepped into the room with Mr. Ali. He looked Connor up and down. "And they call Africa's warlords evil for recruiting child soldiers. But a child bodyguard? That is truly beyond belief."

"I don't kill. I protect," said Connor, his fingers wrapping around the handle of the hidden flare gun.

Oracle chuckled. "Well, you're not doing a very good job, then, are you?"

Connor had no answer for that. He'd been doing his best, but had been betrayed by the very person he was protecting.

"Emily's told us everything about you," explained Oracle, confirming Connor's worst fears. "Quite a little James Bond, aren't we?"

At that, Connor whipped the flare gun from his pocket. But before he could aim it, Spearhead seized his arm in a viselike grip.

"Nice try," he spat in Connor's face, prying the flare gun

from his grasp. Then he stripped him of his go-bag and emptied his pockets.

"And to think I was going to be merciful to you," said Oracle, shaking his head in exaggerated disappointment.

He handed Connor a cell phone.

"Call your people. Tell them you have only twenty-four hours to live."

43

Charley answered her phone on its first ring. "Connor, is that you?"

"Yes—"

"Thank goodness," she said, glancing across at Colonel Black and giving him a thumbs-up. "Listen, there's an Australian warship twelve nautical miles due east of your position. Can you tell me—"

"Charley, you have to listen to me," interrupted Connor, his voice sounding strained. "I've just been captured. I've been given twenty-four hours to live. Emily is . . ."

The line crackled and Connor's voice was lost.

Charley pressed the phone to her ear. "Connor! Are you still there?"

"Hello there, Charley."

She felt her blood run cold at the unfamiliar voice. "Who is this?"

"We have your *guardian*." There was a snort of derision.

"I'm afraid his protection days are over. Unless Mr. Sterling agrees to the ransom demand."

The connection was cut.

Charley stared at her phone, the small hope she'd harbored for Connor ending with the call.

44

Mr. Sterling crossed his arms and stared at Colonel Black. "Well, we can rule out your final ring of defense!"

Charley could hold her tongue no more. "Connor's life's at stake because he risked it trying to protect your daughters!" she exclaimed. "Don't you understand the sacrifice he's made? That Brad has already paid? Are you so pigheaded and self-centered that you can't see we're doing everything in our power to bring back your family? Yet all you can do is criticize and complain. If you were the one with those pirates, I'd leave you there to rot! But it's not you. There are nine loyal crew, your fiancée, your daughters and Connor. You're not helping resolve this crisis. Now either work with us or get out!"

Charley glared at Mr. Sterling, daring him to argue with her. The media mogul stood openmouthed as if he'd been slapped across the face. It was quite apparent no one had ever spoken to him like that before, let alone a teenager.

Colonel Black turned to Charley, not sure whether to be angry or proud. "That's no way to speak to our client."

"Quite right," fumed Mr. Sterling. "I want her gone."

The colonel turned on him, his eyes hard and unforgiving. "No. Charley made a very valid if blunt point. Your attitude, Mr. Sterling, is an obstacle to the success of this ransom negotiation. It could very well get them all killed."

Mr. Sterling swallowed hard, trying to compose himself under the colonel's ferocious glare. He lowered himself back into his chair and clasped his hands together, his expression almost contrite. "No one speaks to me in that way, let alone a child, although I accept that the stress of this situation may have been clouding my judgment." He seemed as if about to apologize. But he didn't. Instead he focused on Colonel Black. "So what's the plan now?"

"We continue to negotiate. Play for time. That's all we can do until I speak with your navy and establish what action—"

Mr. Sterling's smartphone rang. He looked at the display. "It's them."

With Connor's life now at stake, Colonel Black was determined to direct him. "Offer them ten million dollars," he instructed. "That's half the highest ransom paid to date. They'll probably reject it, but it's a decent sum. Shows we're serious. We can work our way up to twenty million."

"But that was for an oil tanker and its crew," retorted Mr.

Sterling, becoming belligerent once more as he pressed the Speakerphone button. "Mr. Ali?"

"Yes. Sorry I missed your call earlier—"

"Is my daughter alive?" demanded Mr. Sterling, ignoring the negotiator's hollow apology.

"Yes, she's shocked but unharmed. I can't guarantee I'll be able to stop Oracle next time, though."

"I want to speak with Amanda and Chloe."

"Maybe later," said Mr. Ali. "Now, let's get down to business before anyone is seriously hurt."

Charley gripped the arms of her chair, listening intently to the call. All she could think of was Connor and Colonel Black's words: *Mistakes can cost lives.*

Whether through arrogance, stubbornness or stupidity, Mr. Sterling decided to continue the negotiations himself. He wet his lips before replying. "I can fly in five million dollars within two days."

Colonel Black glared at Mr. Sterling, but said nothing.

On the phone they heard Mr. Ali sigh. "Mr. Sterling, I thought I'd made myself abundantly clear: one hundred million dollars, nothing less. You should know that, if you do not pay, or are unwilling to, you will leave the pirates no option but to kill Connor and hand your family over to Seven Sabers."

Mr. Sterling's eyes widened in alarm. "The terrorists?"

"That's correct, and those extremists aren't known for their hospitality to Westerners."

"Well, ten million, then."

Mr. Ali didn't reply.

"Plus the yacht. It's worth fifty million alone."

"They already have your yacht. And what use is it to them? Mr. Sterling, I advise you to think very carefully. Oracle has vowed to kill one of the crew for every offer you make below a hundred million. He may even start with your beautiful fiancée."

Mr. Sterling started to answer but then shut his mouth.

"Are you still there? Mr. Sterling?"

"Y-yes . . . I need to speak with my accountant. I'll call you back."

45

Beginner's luck. That's all it had been.

Connor was a fool to think he possessed the skills necessary to be a bodyguard. It was luck that had saved the president's daughter's life that day. Not him. And now good fortune had turned its back on Connor. He was a captive of the pirates, the same as Chloe, Amanda and the *Orchid*'s crew. Just another hostage . . . another liability.

Connor clenched his fists in frustration and despair. He wanted to scream. To tear down the walls of the storage room that was now his prison. Why had he ever thought he could follow in his father's footsteps? What had possessed him to do the very job that had killed his father?

And that would now end his own life.

Failure is the key to success; each mistake teaches us something.

That's what Colonel Black had said. Well, Connor had certainly learned the hard way not to trust his Principals. Not that such knowledge would be of any use to him now. He'd be dead within the next twenty hours—unless Mr. Sterling agreed to pay the ransom. But, based on the man's track record as a ransom negotiator, Connor doubted that would happen in his remaining lifetime. Mr. Sterling was stone-hearted enough to gamble with his own daughters' fate, so from his viewpoint Connor would be expendable. No wonder Emily had turned against her father.

Colonel Black and Charley would, of course, be doing anything and everything to secure his release. But he wasn't the pirates' main prize. He was simply leverage in the negotiations. Like the crew, his life would be sacrificed simply to prove the pirates' resolve.

Connor's thoughts turned to his mum and gran. How would they cope? His mum's health was frail enough as it was. His death might even be the end of her. His gran would tough it out, like she always had throughout her life. But he'd promised to see them both soon. And he never broke his promises to his gran. Connor fought back tears. He realized this would likely be the one promise that he couldn't keep.

The door swung open and Connor looked up. Cali the stowaway appeared with a tray. Behind him stood a hollow-cheeked guard, gun slung across his chest, his mouth chewing lazily on khat leaves.

Cali put the tray down at Connor's feet. There was a steaming bowl of brown mush along with a bottle of water.

"Is this my last meal?" said Connor dryly.

"Goat stew," Cali replied, not meeting his eye. He stood. "I thought you dead."

"What do you care?" snapped Connor. "I should've trusted my gut instinct on the yacht. You're a pirate and a liar. Just like Emily."

"Hadal ma jiro!" barked the guard.

Cali hurried out of the room, and the guard slammed the door shut.

Connor eyed the goat stew, the waft of meat thick in his nostrils. Despite his hunger, he pushed the bowl away. Having seen the animal slaughtered, Connor had no appetite for it. Tomorrow he'd likely be suffering the same fate.

46

Connor stirred. The exhaustion of the past few days had finally caught up with him, and he'd succumbed to sleep. But it was a fitful rest, full of nightmarish visions. Goats with slit throats. Decks awash with blood. Brad's bullet-ridden corpse bloating in the sun. His own body lying next to it, quivering in a death twitch.

His nerves so on edge, Connor snapped awake as soon as he heard the lock turn. The door swung open, and Cali entered.

"You not eat," he said, looking at the untouched bowl of congealing goat stew.

"I can't stomach it," said Connor, "like I can't stomach you."

Cali frowned at him. "I come to get you."

A cold dread seized Connor at the impending execution. Surely it couldn't be that time already. He glanced at his watch. It was only 10:17 p.m. Twenty-four hours hadn't passed. *Does that mean a deal has been struck?* Unlikely in so few hours. In all probability, the pirates were going to torture him to put more pressure on the negotiations.

Connor glanced into the corridor behind Cali. There was no guard in sight. Connor rose to his feet. This might be his last and only chance to escape. He could easily overpower Cali.

"Where's the guard?" asked Connor, preparing to pounce.

"I tell the guard a boat come. More khat for him. Now I guard you."

Smiling, Cali stepped aside from the door, offering Connor no resistance and a way out.

Connor hesitated in his attack. He narrowed his eyes at Cali. No longer did he trust anyone. *Is this a trap? A cruel game to break my spirit?*

When Connor didn't move, Cali took a step forward and unslung a familiar backpack. "Your bag," he said, his expression expectant as he offered it to Connor. "I got all your things. Your flare gun too."

Connor cautiously took it. "Why are you helping me?"

Cali blinked in surprise. "You save my life."

Connor recalled the moment he'd shoved Cali aside as the jug-eared pirate blasted the *Orchid*'s corridor with his AK-47. "You were in my way!"

Cali shrugged. "Still save me."

"But you're one of them."

"I never pirate!" hissed Cali, bitterness in his voice.

"I don't believe you."

"I have no choice," said Cali, showing him his scarred arms. "They whip me if not."

He glanced nervously toward the open door. "Guard be back soon. I hear bad things. They not release your friends. No one."

"What do you mean?" exclaimed Connor. "Not even if the ransom is paid?"

Cali shook his head. "They hand them to Seven Sabers. White man order it."

Seven Sabers? A white man? Connor was confused, as well as troubled, by this development.

"You in great danger," urged Cali. "We go now. There are skiffs on port side. We take them. We escape."

Connor searched the boy's eyes for any hint of deceit. But he saw none. Against his better judgment, he decided he had to trust Cali with his life. After all, what other choice did he have?

47

Connor waited in the shadows as Cali approached the guard from the other end of the corridor. Connor recognized him as the jug-eared pirate from the yacht. He was dozing, slumped against the wall, his arms wrapped around his AK-47 like a pillow. The pirate roused at Cali's approach and stood up. He muttered something. Cali smiled innocently and produced a handful of green stems. Grunting in satisfaction, Juggs snatched the fresh khat from Cali's grasp. As he picked through the leaves, Connor crept up behind.

His rescue plan relied on stealth, cunning and a great deal of luck. Cali was opposed to the idea, but Connor refused to leave the ship without Chloe, at the very least, under his protection.

Despite his nerves, Cali kept the pirate's attention focused on him by chatting and pointing out the choicest leaves.

Connor got within ten paces . . . then five . . . three . . .

two . . . He pressed the barrel of his flare gun into the small of the pirate's back.

"Gacmaha madaxa saara," said Connor, repeating the Somali phrase Cali had taught him.

The pirate froze, then dropped the khat and obediently raised his hands. Cali grabbed the AK-47 before unlocking the door to the captain's cabin. With a prod from his gun, Connor directed the pirate inside.

A middle-aged Japanese man in a creased and dirty captain's shirt was startled from his sleep on the sofa. Switching on a table lamp, he scrambled for his glasses.

"Nani? What's happening?" he demanded, blinking in astonishment at the teenage boy holding the pirate at gunpoint.

Connor tossed the captain a roll of gaffer tape that he'd taken from the storage room. "Quick. Bind him."

Without needing to be told twice, the captain bound Juggs's wrists, torso and ankles, and lastly taped up his mouth, pinning his ears back in the process. He then rolled him onto the floor, where Juggs lay as helpless as a trussed-up turkey. The pirate, wrestling against his bonds, shook with fury when he saw that he'd been duped by a boy with a flare gun.

Connor pocketed the weapon. The plan had worked; luck had once more been on his side.

The captain frowned at Connor. "I'm Captain Takayama. Are you the rescue party?" he asked dubiously.

"Sort of. I'm Connor Reeves. Chloe and Emily's bodyguard."

If the captain was surprised, he didn't show it. "You certainly have courage, young man. But where's the rest of your team?"

"This is it," admitted Connor. "Where are the girls?"

The captain pointed to an adjoining door. "One of them is in my quarters with Ms. Ryder. The other was taken by the pirates to speak with her father."

"That'll be Emily," said Connor as he opened the door to the bedroom. He heard someone sleepily protest in the darkness. "Chloe! Amanda! Get up. It's Connor. We have to leave."

"Connor?" Chloe rushed out and threw her arms around him. "I thought you were dead!"

Connor experienced a moment of déjà vu. He pulled away, wondering whether this was actually Chloe . . . or Emily. He'd confused the twins once before, and he wasn't about to make the same mistake again—not when one was a possible traitor. He studied her face hard, then ran a hand through her hair.

"What?" said Chloe, smiling at his touch.

On her earlobe Connor spotted the telltale mole. He was rescuing the right one.

Connor returned her smile. "Nothing."

Amanda emerged barefoot behind her. For once the supermodel wasn't a picture of unblemished beauty. Her complexion was pale, her hair a mess and her makeup smeared from crying. "Captain Locke said the pirates shot you."

"They did. But my phone saved me." Chloe gave him a perplexed look and Connor added, "It's a long story. Look, we have to go."

Chloe remained rooted to the spot. "What about my sister?" she asked, her voice as fragile as glass. "The pirates took her."

Connor didn't know how to soften the blow. Nor did he have the time to do so. "I suspect she's in league with the pirates. Possibly has been all along."

Chloe's eyes glazed over with shock. "That's insane."

"I know," said Connor. "But when I tried to rescue her, she tricked me and led me into a trap."

Chloe started to argue but saw the harsh truth in Connor's eyes. She sat down on the sofa, struggling to come to terms with her sister's supposed betrayal.

"I'm sorry," said Connor, laying a hand on her shoulder, "but you're my priority now. And we have to get off this ship before they discover we've escaped."

"What's the plan?" Captain Takayama asked.

Connor explained how the pirate skiffs were tethered to the tanker and the HMAS *Melbourne* was currently stationed twelve nautical miles due east. "It'll be a blind run in the dark, but Cali says the skiffs are all equipped with VHF radios, fuel and water. Once we're a few miles clear of the pirates, we'll contact the navy and hope they send help."

"It sounds suicidal," said Amanda. "Why don't we wait until Maddox pays the ransom rather than risking our lives like this?"

"Because the pirates never intend to release us. Cali says we're to be handed to the terrorists—Seven Sabers."

Amanda went deathly quiet.

Captain Takayama took the AK-47 from Cali and flicked off the safety catch. "After nearly six months of being a prisoner, it's time I was a proper captain again. I must rescue my crew . . . and yours. I know where they're being held."

"Cali and I will help," said Connor.

"No, your duty is to these young women. Get them to safety. We'll meet on the port side. If there are any problems, just go. Don't risk your lives waiting for us."

With a bow of respect to Connor, the captain hurried out of the cabin.

48

"I have to get my shoes and belongings first," said Amanda, returning to the bedroom.

"Just your shoes—and hurry," urged Connor, feeling like every second ticking away was another lost opportunity for escape.

The pirate Juggs continued writhing on the floor, but the captain had done his job well, and the bonds held firm. He glared at Connor, then at Cali, his eyes venomous and filled with hate. Connor had no doubt that if the pirate got free, he'd tear them both limb from limb.

"I can't believe my sister would do such a thing," murmured Chloe, looking to Connor to take back his words.

"I'm sorry, Chloe, but I can't deny what I saw—" Connor caught a flash of movement in the doorway. Bucktooth, a bruise purpling his jaw, had just walked in on them, stunned to see Connor free and Juggs held prisoner. Connor rushed to grab him, but this time the pirate boy got to his revolver first.

"Joogso!" said Bucktooth, shoving the gun into Connor's face, his hands trembling ever so slightly as his finger wrapped around the trigger. Connor didn't know if the boy had it in him to actually kill someone, but he wasn't willing to take the risk. Retreating back into the room, Connor raised his hands. So did Chloe.

Bucktooth spoke rapidly to Cali in Somali. Cali's reply sounded to Connor as if he was pleading. He then stepped away, distancing himself from Connor. For all his protests about not being a pirate, the boy was quick to change sides when it suited him. *But can I really blame him?* The boy was a survivalist. In his brutal world, he had to be.

"Hubka dhiga!" said Bucktooth.

"Put your weapons down," Cali translated.

Bucktooth was taking no chances with him this time. Connor slowly withdrew the flare gun from his pocket and dropped it on the floor. The pirate boy dipped the revolver's barrel toward Connor's other pocket and gave another order. Connor obediently reached in and pulled out the slim black tube Bucktooth had spotted.

"It's just a flashlight," explained Connor, holding it up for the boy to see. "Look."

As Bucktooth peered at it, Connor pressed the button, and a glaring green laser shot out. The Dazzler blinded the pirate. Darting forward, Connor leaped on Bucktooth and sent him crashing to the floor. In panic at losing his sight, the boy thrashed wildly, and Connor fought to pin him down. Cali rushed to Connor's aid, grabbing the boy's gun and wrenching it from his grasp. Connor immobilized Bucktooth with a reverse choke. The pirate boy started to shout for help, but Connor applied pressure, and the cry died in his throat as pain racked his body.

"Quick, get the tape," Connor ordered Cali, glad to discover the stowaway was still on his side.

As Cali bound Bucktooth, the pirate boy started to sob. Connor couldn't help but feel sorry for the lad. "Tell him the blindness is only temporary."

Cali spoke quietly and the boy calmed down. Then Cali taped up his mouth.

Amanda peeked around the bedroom door. "Is it safe to come out?"

"Depends upon your definition of safe," replied Connor, rolling Bucktooth onto his front and leaving him beside the other trussed-up pirate. He picked up the flare gun and Dazzler, pocketing them. Cali armed himself with Bucktooth's revolver. "Time to go."

The four of them hurried from the captain's cabin, Connor taking a moment to lock the door. Then they dashed along the corridor to the main stairwell. Connor was about to lead them down, when he heard footsteps and saw Spearhead's bald dome through the metal grilles. The pirate was coming their way.

Doubling back, they discovered another flight of stairs, reaching it just as Spearhead entered the corridor. Descending two flights to the main deck, they arrived at the external door. Connor peered through a porthole. Outside it was pitch-dark, the stars pinpricking the sky. There were no guards in sight.

Connor looked back at Chloe. "Stay close to me."

Chloe nodded. Connor put on his night-vision sunglasses. He'd need every advantage if they were to reach the skiffs without being spotted.

49

"What's with the sunglasses?" hissed Amanda.

"Night vision," whispered Connor, checking through the porthole once more—a good thing, too. In his silvery enhanced vision, he spied a pirate leaning against the rail, smoking a cigarette. He'd been partly hidden behind a stack of oil drums stockpiled to refuel the skiffs. They'd have to wait for him to move on.

A tense minute passed. Still the pirate leisurely puffed away, seemingly unconcerned about holding a lit cigarette beside containers of flammable fuel.

"We can't stay here forever," whispered Amanda, glancing nervously over her shoulder at the cabins behind them, any one of them potentially harboring a pirate.

"I know," said Connor, aware that Spearhead might have discovered Juggs and Bucktooth and already raised the alarm.

Footsteps rang out on the stairwell above.

They couldn't wait any longer.

"What's *hello* in Somali?" Connor asked Cali.

"Iska warran," he replied, bemused.

Connor opened the bulkhead door and strode through the darkness toward the pirate.

"Iska warran," he called out.

The pirate turned to him, expecting a friend. Instead he was blinded by a strobing laser. Connor rushed forward and shoulder-barged the pirate over the rail. The man let out a shocked cry, then tumbled from view. Connor heard a splash and hoped he could swim. Noticing a life ring, Connor tossed it over the side just in case the man couldn't.

Connor glanced along the tanker's port side. Halfway down the deck, he spotted the figure of Captain Takayama. His crew clambered, one at a time, over the gunwale to descend a rope ladder. One of the skiffs was already full. He was too far away to be certain, but Connor thought he recognized two women among the passengers, Sophie and Kathy from the *Orchid*. Which meant Captain Takayama had been true to his word—he'd freed the *Orchid*'s crew too.

Connor beckoned Chloe, Amanda and Cali out.

"Stay underneath the pipework," he instructed. "There may be lookouts on the bridge tower."

After a quick check above, Connor led the dash across the exposed deck to an overhead walkway. They ducked beneath its shelter, then picked their way through the tangle of struts, pipes and metalwork. The going was slow, since only Connor could see well enough in the dark. As he helped Chloe over a pipe, there was a startled movement and strange noise. Amanda let out a scream. Cali stifled it with his hand.

"Goat," he whispered in her ear.

Amanda, her eyes wide, nodded that she understood and Cali removed his hand. But the damage had been done: her cry had caught the attention of a pirate. Through the lattice of pipes, Connor saw someone approaching on the walkway above. He signaled to the others to stay absolutely still. The pirate stopped no more than a few feet from them, his sandals visible through the metal grilles. Connor watched the pirate as he hunted for the source of the sound. His eyes passed over them, but evidently he didn't see them in the darkness. Then the pirate heard the goat bleat, a forlorn cry for its missing companion. The pirate spat at the beast, then shouted some abuse before walking away.

Farther along the deck, Connor noticed Captain Takayama glance in their direction. He'd heard the pirate shouting and now hurried the last of his crew over the side before following them down the ladder himself.

"They're going to leave without us!" gasped Amanda, abandoning their hiding place.

"No! Wait!" hissed Connor.

But Amanda had already bolted. She ran out onto the deck, putting herself in full view of the pirate. Connor prayed the man wouldn't turn her way. Amanda reached the rail and was climbing over when a blaring alarm shattered the night and the tanker was suddenly ablaze with light.

50

Connor grabbed Chloe's hand to make a run for it. But the pirate came charging back down the metal gantry overhead. He saw Amanda and raised his AK-47.

"Joogso!"

He shot at her, bullets peppering the deck, just as she dropped down over the side and into the skiff below.

With their escape route cut off, Connor hurriedly led Chloe and Cali around a storage tank to the opposite side of the ship. Pirates were now rushing onto the main deck. Some started firing over the port side. Connor could hear the roar of outboards as the two skiffs powered away.

With a sinking heart, Connor realized that Captain Takayama and Captain Locke had been left with no choice but to abandon them. The Japanese captain had said himself, "If there are any problems, just go."

"What do we do now?" said Chloe, cowering in the shelter of a pump. "We have no way to get off this ship."

Connor glanced along the tanker's starboard side. The gangway was still down. "The pirates think we're on the skiffs. We need to get to the *Orchid*."

"Do you know how to pilot it?" asked Chloe. "I certainly don't."

"No. But the tender's ready to launch."

The alarm ceased. Only the crack of gunfire now punctured the night. Spearhead appeared on deck, barking commands at the pirates to pursue the hostages.

"Let's go," said Connor.

Stepping from the cover of the storage tank, they sprinted along the deck toward the gangway. Suddenly gunfire burst around their feet. Connor pulled Chloe into his protection and dived behind a control box. Cali dropped down next to them. More bullets pinged off the metalwork.

"Joog halkaaga!" screamed a pirate.

"He say to stay where we are," whispered Cali, his eyes white with fear.

"As if we have another choice," Connor muttered, peering around the control box. Pirates were closing in from all sides. They were pinned down. Just as he'd been in his Guardian training exercise only a month before. But this time the bullets were real. And this time any mistake meant certain death.

As before, his next move would be crucial. He shook off any sense of tunnel vision, making certain to look everywhere for threats. In the daylight brightness of the tanker's halogen floodlights, Connor spotted a pirate positioned by the oil drums, another on the walkway overhead and two sneaking down the port side, concealed by the network of pipes. Oracle was on a gantry overlooking the main deck. Emily was with him, Mr. Ali holding a gun to her head.

Over the ship's loudspeaker, the pirate leader announced, "Give yourselves up, or the girl dies!"

Chloe locked eyes with Connor. "We have to surrender."

"They won't shoot her," Connor insisted. "Whether Emily's one of the pirates or not, she's more valuable to them alive than dead."

"I'll give you to the count of five," said Oracle, his fury evident in his tone.

Chloe grabbed Connor's arm. "How can you be so sure? They killed Brad!"

Connor couldn't be sure.

"Five . . ."

"Emily could've been forced to trap you. Tortured. Anything!" cried Chloe, becoming more and more distraught.

Connor realized he was taking a huge gamble by assuming Emily was one of the pirates.

"Four . . ."

"The Emily you describe isn't the one I know," continued Chloe. "She's my twin sister. We have to save her."

"Three . . ."

Chloe went to stand, but Connor pulled her back down behind the control box. "You may be right. But we're not surrendering. The pirates never intend to release you."

"Two . . ."

"My job is to protect you. And I'll fight to save you both."

"One!" shouted Oracle.

Connor drew the flare gun from his pocket, took aim and fired.

51

The flare struck the oil drums, its sparks igniting spilled fuel and causing a massive explosion. The expanding ball of fire engulfed the nearest pirate. His flaming body plummeted like a comet over the side, the fire extinguished in the sea below.

The force of the explosion then ripped across the deck. Pirates dived for cover. The gantry above rocked on its supports, knocking Oracle and Mr. Ali off their feet. Emily, thrown against the rail, hit her head and was laid out cold.

As the pirates reeled from the blast, Connor broke from behind the control box and over to the port side. He pulled Chef's Molotov cocktail from his go-bag, found his lighter, lit the fuse and tossed it. The bottle shattered on impact, spreading a river of fire across the deck. The two pirates there fled from the flames. The pirate on the walkway didn't know which way to turn as chaos reigned around him. The Molotov's flames reached another set of oil drums.

Connor darted back to Chloe and Cali as the fuel in the oil drums ignited with a roar.

"Run!" he shouted.

He felt his skin being scorched from the heat of the blast. He tried to shield Chloe as they sprinted for the gangway, the smell of her singed hair in his nostrils.

"Connor, you crazy!" screamed Cali, running for all he was worth.

Flames seemed to lick at their heels. Thick black smoke swirled around them. They reached the top of the gangway as the blast from the drums at last subsided.

Chloe stopped, panting hard, her face smeared with sweat and smoke. "What about my sister?"

Connor was caught in a dilemma. He couldn't leave Chloe unprotected, yet he had a duty to rescue Emily, even if she was helping the enemy. Now more than ever he wished he had Ling at his side.

Connor looked to Cali. Once more he'd have to trust the Somali boy. But this time with Chloe's life.

"Get Chloe to the tender garage. If anyone comes, hide in the bilge."

Cali nodded. "I guard her," he said, holding up Bucktooth's revolver. "With my life."

Connor hoped Cali wouldn't have to put that claim to the test, but he admired the boy's courage. He grinned. "We'll make a bodyguard of you yet."

52

The tanker rocked with another explosion. Louder. Deeper. And more ominous. Whatever chemicals were aboard the ship, they were now igniting.

Connor rushed across the deck. With the tanker ablaze, the pirates were panicking, more concerned with abandoning the ship than stopping him. Black smoke billowed in the air, obscuring the halogen lights and turning the scene into a hellish twilight, the fires flickering orange red.

Connor fought his way through the flames and up the stairs to the gantry. Emily still lay on the metal decking. He prayed she wasn't seriously hurt. Or worse, dead.

"Emily!" he called, running over.

She didn't respond.

Kneeling down beside her, he put his fingers to the pulse in her neck.

"You've cost me millions!"

Connor spun around. Oracle stood behind him, the tanker's flames reflecting in his silver-mirrored glasses. He aimed his gun at Connor's chest.

"A hundred million dollars, to be exact. And you'll pay for it with your life."

Oracle pulled the trigger. The gun blast rang in Connor's ears. At the same time he felt the devastating impact of the bullet and was thrown backward over Emily's body. He lay across her, stunned and immobile. Then he took a heaving gasp for breath. His T-shirt and top had withstood the handgun's attack. But he'd been winded badly, and his chest throbbed from another blunt trauma.

Oracle cocked his head to one side when he realized Connor wasn't dead. Then he spotted the compacted lead shot that had dropped into Connor's lap.

"Bulletproof clothing?" He laughed. "Now, that is something I need."

Through the haze of pain, Connor frantically reached for the Dazzler in his pocket. His flare gun was useless, since he hadn't reloaded it. He fumbled for the flashlight, but his body was still in shock from the bullet's impact, and he dropped it.

"Well, at least I get the pleasure of killing you twice," said Oracle, raising his gun. "I'll shoot you in the head this time, though. Just to make sure."

Connor's fingers found the Dazzler. Too late.

A shot rang out.

Connor recoiled, expecting to die. But it was Oracle who fell to the ground, a bullet through his head.

Connor blinked, disbelieving what he saw.

A white man stood on the gantry, flames like hellfire rising up behind him. He seemed completely unperturbed by the destruction and panic around him. His face was a mask, no emotion, no color, his skin pale as ash.

The man pointed his gun at Emily. "Does she live?"

Connor nodded, trying to shield her with his body.

The man studied Connor a moment, his gaze as pitiless and cold-blooded as a snake's.

A third explosion shook the tanker to its core, and a cloud of black smoke enveloped the gantry. Connor coughed, his eyes stinging from the chemical fumes. He heard a voice, disturbingly close, whisper something about "a little sparrow," and then Emily spluttered for breath.

When the smoke cleared, the man was gone.

53

Wincing from the bruising on his chest, Connor lifted the semiconscious Emily onto his shoulders. Another detonation rumbled through the tanker. The gantry lurched sideways. Connor staggered across to the stairwell. His heart pumping, smoke clogging his lungs, he carried her down to the main deck. Only now did Connor fully appreciate his instructor Steve's fitness training.

In an emergency, you'll need such strength to get you and your Principal out of the danger zone.

Connor just hoped he could muster enough. His body had taken a serious battering over the past few days. He was running purely on adrenaline.

At the foot of the stairs, he passed the lifeless body of Mr. Ali with a bullet through his head, execution-style.

A pirate raced past screaming, his back in flames as he threw himself over the side.

The tanker's main deck was now a sea of fire. The route to

the gangway seemed impassable. But Connor had no option. He sprinted along the outer edge, the heat so intense that he thought his skin would melt. Acrid smoke swirled in front of his eyes, and he became disoriented. He shot straight past the gangway. Backing up, he stumbled down the steps, Emily now a dead weight on his shoulders. Starved of oxygen and pushed to his limit, Connor felt that his legs might give way at any moment.

Then his feet touched down on the *Orchid*'s stern.

Keeping an eye out for pirates, he rushed toward the aft stairwell, hurried down the steps, and entered the lower deck's corridor. He staggered the last few feet. At the door to the tender garage, he spun the lock, kicked it open and came face-to-face with a gun.

54

"Don't shoot!" cried Connor. "It's me!"

Cali lowered the gun. "Sorry, I thought you pirate."

"Well, you're certainly a bodyguard," said Connor, impressed that the boy had been true to his word. Cali grinned at the praise. Connor carried Emily into the garage. "Where's Chloe?"

"She safe," replied Cali, running over to the bilge hatch.

Chloe emerged, damp and disheveled. "I can't believe you hid in there, Cali, it's revolting." Then she saw her sister. "Emily!"

Emily moaned in pain as Connor lowered her into the tender.

"Is she all right?" asked Chloe.

"I think it's only a concussion," replied Connor, dashing over to the garage's control panel. "Get in quickly and put a life jacket on her."

As Chloe climbed aboard, he slammed the green Open button with the palm of his hand, and the bay doors slid apart. The monstrous noise of the blazing tanker rushed in, more storage tanks detonating like hydrogen bombs. The *Orchid* trembled in the tanker's furious shadow.

Turning a key, Connor initiated the tender's launch into the water.

"Watch out, Connor!" cried Cali, pointing behind him. "It's Big Mouth!"

Connor spun to see a gangly pirate standing in the bulkhead doorway, an AK-47 in his grip. As Big Mouth raised the gun, Connor kicked the door shut on him and threw his weight behind it.

"Hurry!" Chloe shouted as the tender slid down the ramp.

The pirate pounded on the metal door and Connor could no longer hold it shut. He ran for his life and jumped into the boat with the others. As soon as the tender left its mountings and slid into the water, he pressed the ignition and the engine kicked into life.

Big Mouth burst through the doorway and began firing.

"Hold on tight!" Connor shouted, pushing the throttle forward as bullets whizzed overhead and rapped like hail along the boat's hull.

The tender's engines roaring, their boat took off and Big Mouth was left screaming in frustration. Behind them, the tanker burned like an open furnace. It felt as if the heat was chasing them even as they escaped.

The motorboat cut through the water, the waves fire red in the reflected light of the inferno. Gradually the sea darkened as the tanker receded into the distance, and they entered the open water of the Indian Ocean.

55

Through his night-vision lenses, Connor identified Spear-head and Big Mouth crouched in the skiff's bow, their AK-47s tucked against their shoulders. They let loose another volley of shots, then broke from firing to load a new clip.

Connor leaped back into the pilot's seat. Straightening their course, he pushed the throttle into the red zone, and the tender powered away. They thumped over the waves, Chloe, Emily and Cali clinging on for dear life.

The gunfire resumed, and Connor veered left, then right, trying to avoid the bullets.

"They catch up!" shouted Cali.

Connor glanced over his shoulder. The supercharged skiff was gaining on them rapidly.

"What now?" cried Chloe over the strained roar of the tender's engines. "The radio's gone."

Connor reached behind and yanked the tag that activated

the go-bag's SART. The high-powered LED beacon began to flash as the device transmitted its high-powered locating signal.

"What do you think you're doing?" exclaimed Chloe, staring at the flashing light in horror. "Are you trying to make yourself a target?"

Connor didn't have much choice. If he shrugged off the backpack, he'd lose the protection of the liquid body-armor panel. But Spearhead certainly seemed to appreciate the flashing light of the search-and-rescue transponder. The tender rattled with the impact of more direct hits from 7.62 mm high-velocity rounds.

Cali knelt up and took aim with the revolver. But a wave hit the boat hard and he was jolted against the side. He lost his grip on the revolver, the gun clattering over the edge and disappearing into the dark waters.

"Sorry!" Cali despaired, ducking down as Spearhead and Big Mouth continued their assault.

Spray breaking over the tender's bow, Connor steered them blindly into the night. There was nowhere for them to hide in the open ocean. All he could hope for was to outrun the pirates. But the tender's engines were already being pushed to their limit. And still it wasn't enough.

The pirate skiff relentlessly closed the gap.

"Cali, grab the flare gun in my pocket," ordered Connor.

Crawling over the jolting deck, Cali pulled out the gun.

"Spare flares are in the side of my go-bag."

Reaching up, Cali unzipped the pocket and found the clip of flares.

"You need to aim at the rear of the skiff," Connor explained, "where the fuel cans are."

Nodding, Cali loaded the flare gun.

The pirates's skiff was now so close, they could hear Spear-head shouting his vengeance. "I KILL YOU! I KILL YOU ALL!"

"Hold boat steady," demanded Cali.

Connor shot him a disbelieving look. At this speed that was impossible, but he steered as straight a path as he could.

Cali closed one eye, took careful aim and fired. The flare *whoosh*ed across the waves. A bright red trail streaked through the night sky. The flare hit its target, and at the moment of impact, the skiff exploded in a massive ball of flame, obliterating the craft and all on board.

"What on earth did you load?" Connor exclaimed, easing back on the throttle, their pursuer now destroyed.

Cali stared in astonishment at the gun, then at the flaming wreck of the skiff.

"It just a flare," he replied with a shrug.

Then they heard the whirr of rotor blades, and a Seahawk helicopter armed with hellfire missiles thundered overhead.

56

The assassin gazed out of his hotel window at the dusty, war-torn streets of Mogadishu. The building opposite, once the glamorous al-Uruba Hotel, was now a crumbling shell, pockmarked with the scars of gunfire. The bullet holes always held such fascination for the assassin. He could never understand why so many missed their target. He only ever needed one bullet.

He put on a fresh shirt, glad to be rid of all the lingering soot and reek of burned chemicals after his escape from the flaming tanker. He held his fingers up to the light and picked at some residual grime. He hated dirt under his fingernails.

His phone rang. He answered it.

"Status report," the caller demanded, the voice distorted by the encrypted line.

"Mission parameters were met. Mr. Gibb is dead. Files wiped. *Australian Daily* editor silenced. All evidence destroyed."

"But what about the ransom negotiations? Those came to a rather unexpected and premature end."

The assassin continued to pick at his fingernails. "Nothing to be concerned about. The hijacking accomplished what it set out to do. Mr. Sterling is no longer a threat to the organization. The story is buried."

"And the pirates?"

"Dead men tell no tales."

"The Sterling girl lives. Is that a problem for us?"

A trace of a thin smile cut across the assassin's lips. "My little sparrow served her purpose, so I wiped her memory of our encounter before freeing her. She knows nothing that could unbalance Equilibrium."

The caller seemed to weigh his answer, then said, "We lost significant investment and risked unnecessary exposure as a result of Mr. Gibb. Ensure our next investment is secure."

"Of course."

"And, Mr. Gray, don't leave any loose ends."

"I never do."

57

"Nice suntan," smirked Jason as Connor entered Guardian's briefing room with Charley.

Where his fire-retardant clothing hadn't protected him, Connor had suffered first-degree burns escaping the blazing tanker. The skin on his face, arms and hands was still red and sore a week later, but healing well. "Very funny. I must have used the wrong oil," he replied.

Jason laughed. "Welcome back, Connor. Sorry for the drop-bear prank. I honestly didn't think you'd fall for it."

After the turmoil of the past few weeks, Connor had forgotten all about that incident. "Don't worry, I'll get you back one day," he said, grinning.

Ling walked over. At first Connor thought she might hug him. Instead she bumped fists with him.

"I can't believe you blew up a tanker!" she exclaimed. "Why am I never there for all the action?"

"I wish you had been," replied Connor. "I could've seriously used your help."

"I doubt that," said Marc. "I heard the fire was seen over twenty miles out at sea."

Connor gave a sheepish grin. "I needed a distraction to rescue the girls."

"Some distraction!" Marc replied, holding up his hand and high-fiving him.

"So who's picking up the bill?" asked Amir, patting his friend gently on the shoulder.

Charley produced a letter headed with the official logo of Sempaku Shipping. "Connor will be glad to learn that the shipping company's insurance covers that little fireworks display."

Amir frowned. "I meant for all the gear I lent Connor and he managed to destroy."

"Hey, it wasn't my fault your smartphones aren't bullet-proof," pleaded Connor.

Amir sighed in exasperation. "You're making a habit of getting shot. Perhaps we should just wrap you in a bullet-proof bag?"

"Good idea," said Richie. "Then you could cover his ugly head!"

"Make sure Richie's bag is double-layered," shot back Connor. "Seriously, though, Amir, your tech kit was a life-saver. I couldn't have succeeded without it."

"Connor's right," said Colonel Black, striding into the briefing room. "The success of an operation doesn't rely on a single bodyguard. It's the work of a whole team. Without the SART in his go-bag, Connor and his Principals would have been recaptured by the pirates and most likely died."

"Well, I'm sure glad I stayed in wet and windy Wales, then," said Amir, but Connor could see he was beaming with pride at the colonel's praise.

As Alpha team took their seats for the debrief, Connor asked, "Do you have any news about Emily?"

The colonel nodded. "I just received the report. It appears her somewhat *unusual* behavior was the result of brainwashing, carried out during her captivity last year. The perpetrators of that kidnapping and this hijack must be linked—possibly as a way to extort money from Mr. Sterling, or to gain control over him or his media companies, or both. But all this is speculation."

"Has Emily been able to shed any light on it?" asked Charley.

The colonel shook his head. "Even though we have proof of her communications from the photos she posted on Instagram, she doesn't remember anything about contacting the pirates. Nor does she recall locking Connor up. The knock to her head may have caused amnesia. But the doctor thinks she may never have been fully conscious of her actions in the first place."

"How can that be?" asked Ling.

"Her captor could have programmed subliminal suggestions into her mind, hypnotism being the most likely method."

"That's freaky," muttered Richie. "I hope nobody ever plays with my brain like that."

"No chance," said Ling. "They'd have to find it first."

Colonel Black silenced her with a stern look. "The good news is that Emily is on the mend. Her doctor says she's responding well to treatment."

"Who do you think is behind all this?" asked Jason.

"It has to be an international crime syndicate. There are several possibilities, but no firm leads."

"What about the man I saw on the tanker?" asked Connor. "Cali said he was the one ordering the handover to Seven Sabers."

The colonel sighed. "Your description of him was pretty vague. There's been no trace of him. We can only assume he died in the blaze."

Connor wasn't so sure. The man had struck him as a shark who could slip any net.

"Anyway, the Australian Federal Police are investigating the hijacking, so it's out of our hands now," announced the colonel. "But Mr. Sterling is deeply grateful to us for rescuing his family, and the crew, *especially* without the need to pay a ransom." Colonel Black raised an eyebrow and gave a wry smile. "As a gesture of his appreciation, he's invited Alpha team to a private party to celebrate his marriage to Ms. Ryder and his daughters' safe return."

"Where's the party?" asked Ling eagerly. "Not on a yacht, I hope."

"Sydney. And we're flying first class all the way."

58

Mr. Sterling had rented an entire island for the party.

Named after its shape rather than its marine life, Shark Island was a unique location for a celebration. It was at the eastern end of Sydney Harbor and boasted spectacular views of the harbor bridge, opera house and Rose Bay. Connor couldn't think of a more ideal setting for a party brimming with famous film stars, musicians, supermodels and high-level politicians. Nor could a location be more secure. Because it was encircled by water, no one could approach the island undetected. And Mr. Sterling hadn't spared any expense on security measures. Besides the high-profile close-protection team patrolling the island, Connor's trained eye had spotted numerous covert bodyguards mingling among the guests.

"Is that who I think it is?" said Ling, nodding toward a suave, dark-haired man in a tailored suit.

Jason nodded. "But he looks a lot shorter than he does in the movies."

"I don't know where to look," sighed Marc as his eyes bounced between all the fashion models sashaying past.

"Don't trip over your tongue, Marc," said Charley, sipping from a glass of sparkling fruit juice.

Chloe and Emily walked toward them, dressed respectively in coral-pink and straw-yellow summer dresses.

"How are you enjoying the party?" asked Chloe.

"It's amazing. Never seen so many famous people," Connor replied. "Thanks for inviting us."

"It's the least we could do." Chloe turned to Ling with a repentant expression. "I hope you can forgive our little disagreement. I realize now you were just doing your job."

"Live and learn, eh?" said Ling coolly.

"We almost *didn't* live," said Emily. "That's why we're so grateful to Connor."

The two sisters exchanged a glance, nodded at some unsaid agreement, then leaned forward and kissed him on either cheek. Connor felt himself blush at the unexpected affection and noticed Charley glance over, then quickly look away. He hoped he wouldn't be in trouble again.

"Hey, I supplied the equipment!" piped up Amir.

The girls laughed and kissed him too. Amir was momentarily lost for words.

Connor studied Emily's face. It seemed like a shadow had been lifted. "You're looking well."

"Thank you, I feel much better," she replied, smiling freely.

"My head was so clouded before, always getting migraines. I thought it was the medication I was on. But that clearly wasn't the case. Now it's like sunshine has broken through. I can think . . . my own thoughts."

Connor returned her smile. "I'm glad you've found yourself again."

He heard his name being called and turned to see a slim African boy among the partygoers. His white silk shirt looked a size too big for him, but he was no longer skin and bones. "Cali! What are you doing here?"

Cali greeted him with a beaming smile. "Mr. Sterling arrange a visa for me."

"I thought you wanted to go to South Africa."

"Yes! Maybe on vacation. I live in Australia now," he replied proudly.

The party went on all afternoon, taking full advantage of the glorious summer sunshine.

Connor and Ling were reunited with the *Orchid*'s crew, Captain Locke even greeting Connor with a salute. The crew members were relaxed and carefree, a world away from the trauma of the hijacking. But Connor noticed they all bore their scars, Jordan's being the most obvious, although he was more than happy to show a glamorous model his "war wounds." The rest of the crew's scars weren't so visible, just the occasional nervous twitch at the sound of a cork popping or Sophie's sad gaze as she looked across the water at the harbor bridge, no doubt thinking of Brad.

As dusk approached, Mr. Sterling and Amanda—his new wife outdoing all the models in an ivory chiffon slit gown—eventually broke from their socializing to thank Connor and the others on Alpha team.

"I always had faith in you, Connor," said Mr. Sterling, warmly shaking his hand and beaming a silvery smile. "Never once doubted that you'd deliver the goods and bring my Amanda and daughters safely home."

"Thank you, sir," replied Connor, although he caught the incredulous look on Charley's face.

Amanda graced him with a kiss, her heady perfume enveloping him as she leaned into his cheek.

"You're one brave boy," she said, ruffling his hair. "If we have a son, I hope he grows up to be like you."

She laid a protective hand over her belly, Mr. Sterling beside her, beaming with pride. Chloe and Emily exchanged surprised looks.

"You're *pregnant*?" asked Chloe.

Amanda nodded. "Twelve weeks."

"Congratulations," said Emily. "That's wonderful news."

As word spread and guests clustered around to toast the new baby, Chloe leaned close to Connor's ear.

"Want to take a ride in our speedboat?" she whispered,

pointing at a sleek red boat moored at the end of the island's jetty.

"Shouldn't we ask your father first?" said Connor.

Chloe glanced at the crowd of well-wishers and shook her head. "No, he's busy celebrating. And he won't mind."

"But what about security?" asked Connor.

"Hey, I have you!" she said, taking his hand. "And Ling can come too."

"Now, that sounds like my sort of fun," said Ling, setting aside her glass of fresh lemonade.

"Emily, are you going to join us?" asked Connor.

"Sure. Why not?" she replied, clearly still trying to take in the news of their pregnant stepmother.

Chloe led the way down to the jetty.

"Want to drive, Ling? It's way faster than a Jet Ski."

Ling grinned. "Definitely. As long as this one doesn't explode!"

Jumping in, Ling settled into the pilot's seat, pressed the ignition and took them out into the harbor. She headed in the direction of the bridge, where the sun was beginning to dip through its arch.

"I can't believe Amanda's having a baby," exclaimed Chloe. "It's the first I've heard about it."

Emily glanced at Connor, then smiled at her sister. "Do you know what? I think I'd really like having a brother."

"Hey, let's see how fast *this* baby goes," said Ling, driving the throttle forward.

The speedboat surged across the harbor, cutting through the water like an arrow. As they zoomed past another boat, Connor did a double take. The boat was being piloted by a bald black man. And in the stern, removing his scuba gear and wet suit, was a white man with a lion tattoo on his arm.

Todd Logan and *Doug Carter*.

The two men watched the Sterlings' speedboat pass by with an unsettling intensity.

Connor's sixth sense went into overdrive. He hunted around the boat.

"What's the matter?" said Emily. "What are you looking for?"

Connor didn't really know until he glanced over the side and found it. On the speedboat's hull, just below the water-line, was a small black box with a transmitter. It could only be one thing.

"Bomb on board!" cried Connor.

The girls stared at him in shock and horror. But Ling re-acted with a bodyguard's instinct. She threw the speedboat's throttle to its max, grabbed Chloe and dived over the side. Connor was a split second behind with Emily in his arms. They hit the water hard, plunging beneath the surface.

A moment later, the speedboat exploded.

59

Connor was sparring with Ling in the Guardian gymnasium when Charley entered and announced, "Good news! Todd Logan and Doug Carter have been caught."

Momentarily distracted by the news, Connor almost got his head knocked off by a roundhouse kick from Ling. He countered with a front kick, then backed away to a safe distance. Amir rang the bell, pausing the boxing-ring timer at one minute and twenty-two seconds remaining. Connor wiped the sweat from his brow while Ling took a slug from her water bottle.

"Where did they find them?" he asked, handing his towel back to Amir.

"It took a while, but the police tracked them down to a guesthouse near Broken Hill in the Australian Outback," Charley replied. "They confessed to planting the bomb. Just as you thought, Connor, Todd attached the device after the security teams had completed their sweep."

"Did they say *why* they did it?" asked Ling.

"For the money. It was just another job, as far as they were concerned."

"Who hired them?" asked Connor.

Charley brought up a photo on her smartphone of a tanned middle-aged man with auburn hair. "Mr. Joseph Ward."

"Mr. Sterling's business rival!" gasped Amir. "The one he exposed for corporate fraud."

"The very same," replied Charley. "Ward blamed Mr. Sterling for destroying his life and family. And he was determined to take his revenge on Mr. Sterling's family. Eye for an eye, tooth for a tooth."

"But isn't he still in jail?" said Ling.

"Yes. And guess where the two ex-cons both served their last sentences? Long Bay Prison. The same prison Ward is being held in."

Amir frowned. "But how did Ward pay them? When I was compiling Operation Gemini's threat report, the papers said all his assets had been seized by the courts."

"As you know, Mr. Sterling has *many* enemies. Not that it surprises me," said Charley, raising an eyebrow. "The disgraced politician Harry Gibb funded the criminal operation."

"But he died of a heart attack," said Connor.

Charley nodded. "Gibb had wanted revenge, for having his illegal dealings exposed by Mr. Sterling's newspapers.

However, he didn't have the necessary criminal contacts—whereas Ward did. Ward's now been charged with *multiple* counts of attempted murder, Todd and Doug having also admitted to sabotaging the Jet Skis."

Connor and Ling exchanged astonished looks.

"Sorry, Connor," said Ling, holding up her gloved hands in apology. "Those dudes *were* in the Seychelles."

"Does this mean Ward was also responsible for the hijacking?" asked Connor.

Charley shrugged. "He denies knowing anything about it. The Australian Federal Police are investigating further, but we may never know the truth. I tell you one thing, though: Chloe and Emily were just innocent victims in this tangle of revenge against their father."

"Those poor girls," said Amir, touching his cheek where they'd both kissed him.

"They didn't do too badly," said Ling. "They had Connor protecting them."

Connor grinned—that was the closest he'd get to a compliment from Ling. He allowed himself a moment to enjoy the feeling. But already Ling had raised her gloves into a fighting stance.

"Come on, hotshot. The round's not over yet."

Amir rang the bell and restarted the timer. Connor needed to be on his guard—Ling *always* won her fights. But if his recent assignment had taught him one thing, it was that Charley's motto was true: *Whether you think you can or think you can't, you're probably right.*

So this time he was determined to win.

The End

Turn the Page for a Sneak Peek at

Book 5: Ambush

Connor was violently awakened by a bag being thrust over his head. As he gasped for breath, the thick black fabric smothering all light, strong hands pinned his arms and legs behind his back. He fought to free himself. But plastic zip ties were quickly fastened around his wrists and ankles, binding him tightly.

"Let me go!" he cried, thrashing wildly in a desperate bid to escape. Wrenched from a deep sleep, his mind was a whirl of confusion and blind panic. Lashing out, his heel struck one of his captors, and he heard a grunt of pain.

More hands seized Connor, yanking him upright. As he was hauled from the room, his sneakers dragging across the carpet, he screamed, "HELP! SOMEONE HELP ME!"

But no one answered his call, his cries muffled by the bag.

All of a sudden Connor was hit by a blast of ice-cold air as his captors bundled him outside. Heart pounding and body trembling from the shock of the attack, Connor knew that if he was to survive this ordeal, he had to get a grip on himself. During his bodyguard training in hostage survival, he'd learned that the first thirty minutes of any abduction were the most dangerous. The kidnappers were on edge and highly volatile.

Although it goes against every human instinct, his instructor Jody had explained, *this is the time to stay calm and stay sharp. Be aware of anything that could provide a clue to your whereabouts or your kidnappers' identity.*

Feet crunched on gravel. *Three sets,* Connor noted, trying in some small way to take control of the situation. He heard the trunk of a car being opened. A moment later he was dumped in the back and it was slammed shut with an ominous *thunk.*

No, it isn't a car, Connor corrected himself. He'd been *lifted,* not dropped, into the luggage compartment. The deep throaty rumble of a powerful diesel engine confirmed his suspicions. *It's a 4×4.*

Wheels spun on gravel as the vehicle roared away. His body flung around, Connor's head struck the rear panel with a crunch. Stars burst before his eyes, and pain flared in his skull. Any last vestiges of grogginess were wiped out in an instant.

Someone must have seen me being taken, thought Connor, his mind now sharp. *Someone will raise the alert.*

The wheels hit pavement. The vehicle banked left before accelerating away fast. With the bag still over his head,

Connor attempted to visualize the route his abductors were taking. He carefully counted off the seconds before the next turn.

Sixty-seven . . . sixty-eight . . . sixty-nine . . . The 4×4 took a hard right. Connor began counting again, building up a crude map in his head. He felt the vehicle rise and fall as they passed over a small bridge. He continued his count . . . *twenty-four . . . twenty-five . . . twenty-six . . .*

Connor was totally baffled by his abduction. Usually it was the Principal, the person he was assigned to protect, who was the target for a kidnapping. Surely his captors had made a mistake. Gotten the wrong person. Besides, he wasn't even on an official mission. Then an uncomfortable truth struck Connor: perhaps his kidnappers had indeed snatched the *right* person.

Crumpled in a heap against the rear panel, Connor shifted position to create a space for his hands. The ties around his wrists and ankles were digging painfully into his flesh, cutting off the circulation. He tried to pull a hand free, but the zip ties were heavy-duty, and the plastic just cut deeper into his skin. No matter how hard he strained, they simply wouldn't break.

At a count of forty-seven, the vehicle swung right. Then barely ten seconds later it bore left. And soon after that, left again. By the sixth turn, Connor's mental map had become a confused mess. It seemed like the 4×4 was going in circles, as if his captors were purposely trying to disorient him. Connor now tried to listen above the noise of the road for any conversation in the vehicle. He hoped to gain some insight into his abductors' identity: accent, language, gender, even a name. But they all stayed disturbingly silent. From this Connor deduced they were professionals. They had to be, to break into Guardian HQ undetected.

Maybe my kidnapping's connected with a previous mission?

The best he could hope for was that his captors intended to ransom him. That way he'd be worth more to them alive than dead. But if they wanted to interrogate him, or use him as a pawn in some political or religious protest, then he'd likely be killed. In that case he would risk an escape attempt.

Whatever his abductors' intentions, he needed to find out as soon as possible—his life could depend upon it.

The 4×4 ground to a halt, and the engine was switched off. The back door opened, and he was manhandled out. A gusting wind sent a chill through his body, his T-shirt offering little protection against the winter freeze. Gripped tightly on either side by his captors, Connor detected the faintest trace of perfume through the bag. Was one of the abductors a woman?

"Where are you taking me?" asked Connor, his voice now steady and calm, hoping that the woman would respond.

But his kidnappers remained tight-lipped as they escorted him away from the 4×4. They moved briskly, not allowing

Connor to find his feet. He heard the soft swish of a door sliding open, a welcoming warmth embraced him, and the ground changed from pavement to cushioned carpet. As he was borne deeper into the building, Connor caught the aroma of frying onions and the distant clatter of pots and pans. Heading away from what he presumed was a kitchen, he was dragged several more paces before being shoved into a chair. Its hard wooden slats dug painfully against his bound hands, but at least he could plant his feet on the floor. Connor tried to sit up straight to maintain some dignity before his anonymous enemies, at the same time readying himself to spring into action at the first opportunity.

The place he'd been brought to was oddly quiet, indicating that other people were there with him.

When nobody spoke, Connor demanded, "Who are you? What do you want with me?"

"It's not about what we want," a man's voice replied. "It's about what *you* want."

The BODYGUARD Missions

ACKNOWLEDGMENTS

The "ransom" for completing this fourth installment in the Bodyguard series was paid in blood, sweat and tears by:

Brian Geffen, my editor at Philomel Books, who once again supercharged this edition to ensure my American readers experienced the best possible version of the story.

Michael Green, Publisher, whose undying enthusiasm for the Bodyguard series has made big waves into the book market.

Laurel Robinson, my copy editor, whose keen eye made the final edit plain sailing.

And of course you, my wonderful readers who have followed Connor on two assignments now. I hope you have the nerve and guts to keep by his side during his next mission in Africa. I warn you, it's going to be a deadly ride!

Read, enjoy and stay safe!
Chris

Any fans can keep in touch with me and the progress of the Bodyguard series on my Facebook page, or via the website at www.chrisbradford.co.uk

© Rune Hellestad

Chris Bradford (www.chrisbradford.co.uk) is a true believer in "practicing what you preach." For his BODYGUARD series, Chris embarked on an intensive close protection course to become a qualified professional bodyguard. His bestselling books, including the Young Samurai series, are published in over twenty languages and have garnered more than thirty children's book award nominations internationally. He is a dedicated supporter of teachers and librarians in their quest to improve literacy skills and provides free teachers' guides to his books on his website. He lives in England with his wife and two sons.

Follow Chris on Twitter @youngsamurai.